Mrs. Harvey Becker

KINNERY CAMP

KINNERY CAMP

A Story of the Oregon Woods

Story and Pictures
By
CHARLOTTE BAKER

New York DAVID McKAY COMPANY, Inc. *Publishers*

This book is dedicated to the beautiful state of Oregon and to all my friends there.

CONTENTS

KINNERY CAMP

I

NO PLACE FOR KIDS

"IT'S getting dark," Jeff said.

"It's still daylight," his mother answered. "It just seems dark to us because we are under the big trees."

"Ouch!" cried Joe. "This wagon seat is harder than it was when we started. How much farther is it to Kinnery Camp?"

The driver of the wagon clucked to his team. The two big gray draft horses pulled as hard as they could up the steep road. Besides the driver and the three passengers, the wagon was loaded with sacks of potatoes and apples, and boxes of all kinds of groceries. There was something else, too, that Jeff had been wondering about all the way from town: a mysterious black box of an unfamiliar shape. Jeff wondered whose

11

it was, and what was inside. He couldn't even guess.

The driver answered Joe's question. "Not far."

"*How* far?" Joe persisted.

"Cat's fur, dog's fur; what do you want to know fur?" said the driver.

Jeff giggled. He liked the driver and thought his jokes were funny. Joe was different. He thought the driver was making fun of him, so he went into the sulks.

Their mother said, "We'll be there in time for supper. That will make us all feel better."

"They will be waiting for *you* to cook the supper, Mrs. Kinnery," the driver told her. "When the Boss gave out the news that a real sure 'nuff female cook was coming to camp tonight, the men that were helping dropped everything in the middle of the floor. The Boss, he cussed and he hollered, but he couldn't get nobody to touch the cookstove with a ten-foot pole. Those lumberjacks will all be lined up in the road waiting for you with their mouths watering."

Mrs. Kinnery sighed, thinking of having to cook for thirty men after the long day's ride. Then she cheered up. "Well, anyway, I'm glad they're expecting us."

"They're expecting *you,* Mrs. Kinnery. Not the kids. The Boss said I was to bring you back in the wagon with the supplies. He didn't say nothing about the kids."

12

"Well, of course I'm bringing the boys!" Mrs. Kinnery exclaimed. "Maybe I didn't mention them in my letter, but Boss Kinnery ought to know I wouldn't go off and leave them in town, for pity's sake! I'm his own brother's widow. Joe and Jeff are his own brother's boys. What else *would* I do but bring them with me?"

"Well, I don't know," said the driver doubtfully. "I guess it will be all right. But the Boss, he likes things his own way."

Mrs. Kinnery sat up straight and stuck up her chin. "I've known Boss Kinnery for more years than I care to count, and I've seen some times when he didn't get his own way."

"He's not an easy man to get along with."

She stuck her chin up higher. "Well, he likes to eat, doesn't he? As long as I can cook and he can eat, we'll get along."

Jeff wasn't worried about getting along with his uncle. He liked everybody, and as far as he knew, everybody liked him. He looked forward to getting acquainted. In the meantime, he gazed around him at the big trees.

The road which wound among the trees was so narrow at times that Jeff could hold out his hand and touch the trunks. They were great yellow pines, every one of them thicker than the width of the wagon. They were so tall and straight that Jeff got a crick in his neck

13

from looking up to see the tops. The boughs formed a roof way up above his head. He could hardly see a speck of sky to tell whether the sun had set. The whole forest smelled spicy and sweet. The air was cold, although it was still summer. As the road climbed higher and higher, the air grew sharper and colder.

"Here we are!" the driver announced.

They came out in a large clearing. The trees had been cut down, leaving hundreds of big stumps. The sky was still light, but lamps were burning in the bunkhouses—half-a-dozen of them in a row facing the long frame cookhouse. The road ran between them, and on each side of the road the lumberjacks stood waiting, just as the driver had said they would be. The

15

driver stopped the wagon and some of the men came forward to help him unload.

"Where's Uncle Boss?" Jeff asked.

Mrs. Kinnery looked around. "There he is, standing on the cookhouse steps." She called out, "Good evening, Boss! Here we are."

"Why doesn't he say something?" Jeff wondered. "He just stands there and looks at us. Hello, Uncle Boss!"

Boss Kinnery looked at them as if he couldn't believe his eyes. He was a big, strong man with red hair, frowning like a thundercloud. At last he came up to the wagon. "Hello, Polly," he said. "Whose kids are these?"

Mrs. Kinnery answered sharply, "They're mine, of course, as you very well know!"

"What do you mean by bringing them here?"

Mrs. Kinnery thrust her chin up at him. He was about twice her size. "You hired me to cook, didn't you?"

He glared at her. "Yes, but I didn't say anything about bringing a nursery with you!"

A nursery! Jeff was shocked. He spoke up. "I'm nearly ten years old, Uncle Boss, and Joe is twelve going on thirteen. We can do a lot of work. We're not a nursery!"

His uncle said, "You hush up. I'm talking to your mother. Polly, they'll go back to town tomorrow."

16

"They'll do no such thing!" Mrs. Kinnery cried. "What's the matter with you, Boss Kinnery, that you can't make room for your own brother's children? They'll earn their keep, I promise you!"

Boss Kinnery growled, "I've got nothing against them. But a logging camp is no place for kids. They'll be into everything. You know I want to help you out, Polly, and I'm willing to pay you good wages. Send 'em back to town. They'll be better off there."

Mrs. Kinnery shook her head. "No, sir! If I stay, they stay."

He turned away. "All right. You can *all* go back to town tomorrow, then. I'll hire another cook. A bachelor! You can sleep in the rooms behind the kitchen tonight; they're all fixed up for you."

Jeff and Joe helped their mother with the bags. Joe was so angry and Jeff was so puzzled that neither of them could say a word. As they started into the cookhouse, one of the men said, "But Boss! What are we going to eat?"

"We'll just have to cook for ourselves a while longer. Ole and Mac and Fred—it's your turn in the cookhouse tonight."

"No, py yimminy," Ole said. "Ay vill not cook no more. Ay got a stomach-ache from last time." He was a tall, thin Scandinavian with a mournful face. He looked as if he had not had a good meal for years.

17

"No more dishes for me," Mac spoke up. "I got to take care of my hands." The men laughed. Mac's hands were enormous, with knobby knuckles and thick calluses from a lifetime of using an ax.

Fred added his protest. "You promised to hire us a cook, Kinnery. Well, here she is, and I'll bet she's a good one, too. I for one will quit the job before I work another day without some decent grub!" Fred turned to the other men. "How about that?"

The men murmured and nodded. "Me, too!" "That's right!" "You bet!" they cried.

Boss Kinnery looked at them. He knew that they meant what they said. They had been eating half-cooked beans, heavy biscuits, and bitter coffee ever since the camp cook left two weeks ago.

He turned hopefully to Mrs. Kinnery. "How about cooking for us tonight, anyway, Polly? Now that you're here."

"No, sir," she said. "No kids, no cooking."

Boss's face grew as red as his hair. He waved his arms. "I give up!" he sputtered. "Keep the kids. But don't blame me if they get into trouble. And now for goodness' sake, let's have some food." He stamped off.

Jeff looked after him, wondering why his uncle didn't want him and Joe to stay. He felt very unhappy. For a minute he was afraid he was going to cry, but he couldn't do that with all those men watching him.

18

Joe was frowning as hard as his uncle. He was large for his age, and with his red hair and his frown he looked a great deal like him. "Let's go back to town," he said to his mother.

"Oh, no!" said Mrs. Kinnery. "We came up here to work, and we're *going* to work. It'll take more than your Uncle Boss to keep us from earning an honest living. Come on! Let me see, now, which bag did I put my aprons in?" As she bustled up the steps she spoke over her shoulder to the men. "All right, gentlemen, come back in an hour and you shall have something worth eating."

The hungry lumberjacks slapped one another on the back and cheered.

2

APPLE-KNOCKERS

JEFF AND JOE woke up next morning at five o'clock. They did not wake early because they wanted to, but because their mother called them to help with breakfast. It was so cold that once out of bed they lost no time in getting dressed.

Mrs. Kinnery already had a roaring fire in the stove. "Get some water from the barrel and put it on the stove to heat," she said to Joe. "Jeff, get busy and set the table."

So the day began. Jeff went out on the front steps to call the men when breakfast was ready. He beat as hard as he could on the triangle hanging there, making a wonderful racket. Almost at once the men came stamping into the cookhouse, and then everyone was busy. The men were busy eating; Mrs. Kinnery was busy dishing up the food; and Jeff and Joe were busy carrying it to the table.

"Let me at the hen-fruit!" one of the men called to Jeff, as he passed a platter of eggs. Jeff giggled. Another said, "How about some of those liver pads?" Jeff and Joe looked at each other, puzzled. What in the world were liver pads? "I-I don't think we have any of those," Jeff stammered. "Liver pads! Saddle blankets! Flap-jacks!" explained the man, impatiently. "What's the matter, don't you speak English?"

Joe passed the flapjacks. But their troubles were not yet over. Next, the men were asking for "skid-grease." "You can't eat liver pads without skid-grease, you know!" Mac teased them. This time Jeff caught on and passed the butter. It was like a guessing game. Jeff and Joe were kept fairly hopping from the stove to the table.

Boss Kinnery sat at the head of the table. He was still frowning, but after he had eaten a stack of flapjacks, four eggs, a plate full of potatoes, a slab of bacon, half-a-dozen cookies, and three cups of coffee, he began to look more pleasant. Everyone was nearly through eating, so Jeff and Joe had a chance to stand still for a few minutes. The room was warm and cozy. Jeff blinked. He felt himself growing sleepier and sleepier. The coffee pot he was holding grew heavier and heavier. He

21

nodded. His eyelids closed; all sounds faded away.

The coffee pot tipped and the coffee poured out, splashing all over the scrubbed floor. A growl from Uncle Boss woke Jeff abruptly.

"What are you doing, wasting good coffee!"

Uncle Boss was cross again. He rose and stamped out of the room.

"He doesn't like us," Jeff said sadly.

"You boys will just have to *make* him like you," his mother said. "People will like you if you're worth liking. But sometimes it takes a while." She shook her head. "And I'm afraid you've made sort of a bad start!"

There was still a lot of work to do in the cookhouse. The table had to be cleared; the dishes had to be washed; the table had to be set all over again for supper. Jeff and Joe worked like beavers. They were in a hurry to finish so that they could go outdoors.

When the last place was set they started for the door. "Come back here!" Mrs. Kinnery called. "You have to peel the potatoes!"

"We want to go outside!" Joe complained.

"So do I!" snapped his mother. "But I have to pack

lunches for thirty men instead. All you have to do is peel a few potatoes!"

A few potatoes! When Jeff saw that bucket full of potatoes, his heart sank right down into his shoes. It was so big that he and Joe together could hardly carry it out to the front steps. Mrs. Kinnery gave them a big empty bucket, too. "Put the peeled potatoes in this one," she told them. "And be sure you don't spill the peelings around. And remember—*thin* peelings!"

"Well, we're outside, anyway," Jeff said. "We can see the whole camp from right here. We can see everything that goes on—if there *is* anything going on."

The sun had climbed up to the tops of the trees at the edge of the clearing and it shone down on the steps where the boys sat. They could see where the road forked just beyond the tents where the men lived. One fork led off into the woods; the other went straight on to the corral, where the two big, old, gray draft horses stood looking at Jeff and Joe. There was a barn and a small shed outside the corral. Not a soul was in sight, but a loud, musical banging noise came from the shed.

"What's that?"

"Let's go see!"

They were halfway down the steps when Jeff remembered the potatoes. "We can't go. We got to peel 'em."

24

"Why should we peel Uncle Boss's old potatoes?" Joe grumbled.

"We're not peeling 'em for Uncle Boss; we're peeling 'em for Mamma."

"Oh, all right!" Joe knew that Jeff was right, but that didn't make him any happier. They sat down again and began to peel.

"If only potatoes didn't have dimples!" said Jeff. "It's so hard to peel around their dimples."

Joe scoffed. "Those are their eyes."

"But potatoes grow under the ground. What do they need with eyes?" Joe did not think this was worth answering, so Jeff went on talking to himself. "Maybe they can see in the dark! Maybe they lie there in the kitchen at night and see everything. Just suppose there was a burglar, and he broke into the house one night, and stole all our money and jewels—"

"We haven't got any jewels. Or any money, either!" Joe said.

"Well, just suppose we did. The burglar would steal 'em, and nobody would see the burglar but the potatoes. So when the burglar tiptoed out through the kitchen, the potatoes would all roll out of their sacks and off the shelf and fall, plunk! right on the burglar's head. And—"

"You'd better get to work!" Joe interrupted. "We never will fill that blasted bucket!"

Jeff looked at the bucket. It was still almost empty. And the other bucket was still almost full. He settled down to work. But the bucket seemed to fill very slowly. "Let's put it behind us," Jeff suggested, "Then we won't have to look at it until it's full."

They put the bucket on the top step and turned their backs upon it. The sun climbed higher; the day grew warmer; the full bucket grew emptier; the empty bucket grew fuller—and the peelings grew thicker.

At last they turned around and saw the bucket full of nice white potatoes. Their mother came to the door. "Pick up those peelings!" Wearily Jeff and Joe gathered up the peelings they had dropped. Mrs. Kinnery shook her head, looking at them. "I'd better throw away some of the potatoes and cook the peelings," she said. She looked at the boys standing on the edges of the steps as if they were just about to fly away. "You can play around a while now, if you want to," she told them. "But don't go far. I've got another job for you."

"Another job! Another job!" Joe grumbled as they walked along the road. "I've had enough jobs to last me for a while. When I grow up I'm going to Alaska and get me a gold mine. Then I'll just drive my dog team around in the winter and fish in the summer. I won't ever work any more."

"When I grow up I'm going to work in the woods like Uncle Boss," Jeff said. "But *I'll* be *glad* when my

26

nephews come to live with *me*."

They had come to the shed where the noise of hammering was still going on. They looked in the open door. A short, square man stood at an anvil, hammering a piece of iron. He lifted the big hammer and brought it down with a grunt. His arms were very long and knotted with muscle; he had a chest like a barrel and a bulging stomach, but his legs were very short. "Hi!" he said to the boys. "Come on in, if you want."

"Hello, Mister—" Jeff said, as they entered the shack.

"Just call me Shorty," the blacksmith said. "They call me Big Shorty, because there's another Shorty in the outfit. He's shorter than I am, and skinny to boot, so they call him Little Shorty. Did you just make your getaway from the cookhouse?"

"Yes. We had to peel potatoes," Joe said.

"I'm glad we're through with potatoes," Jeff added.

"You ain't through with the potatoes. You'll never be through with potatoes. We eat 'em three times a day."

"Ohhhh!" groaned the boys.

"Your ma's a good cook. I never ate better cackleberries and java. I always say anybody that can turn out good cackleberries and java is a good cook."

"Cackleberries?" Jeff wondered.

"Don't you know what cackleberries are? What happens when the hen cackles?"

27

"Oh, yes! Eggs!"

"Sure. You'll catch on. You're not doing so bad for a couple of young apple-knockers."

"What's an apple-knocker?"

"Oh, apple-knockers are folks that live in the valley. They don't know how to do nothing but knock apples out of trees. They don't know their way around in the big woods. Well, I'm about ready to shoe that horse."

Joe jumped for the door. "Let me bring the horse out!"

Big Shorty looked him over. "Think you can handle him? Besides, you don't even know which one I want."

"Sure I can! Sure I do! He's the one with the shoe off his left hind foot. He's got a white streak down his nose and a lot of black hairs in his tail."

Jeff looked at Joe admiringly. He hadn't noticed any of those things. Big Shorty looked surprised. "Hmm!" he said. "All right, bring him out."

Jeff held the gate open while Joe went in with a halter and approached the two horses. They turned their heads toward him and pushed forward their ears. They were so big and so heavy that Jeff was a little bit afraid of them, though he wouldn't have said so for the world. He was glad to be near the gate.

Joe wasn't afraid. He never seemed to be afraid of anything. He put out his hand and rubbed the nose with the white streak on it. The horse gave him a

28

playful push that almost knocked him down. "Now, look here, horse," Joe said, "pick on somebody your size!" He kept talking to him and rubbing his nose. In a few minutes the horse was putting his head down to get his ears scratched, and Joe slipped the halter on. Then he led him out of the gate, which Jeff closed behind him.

29

Joe held the horse while the blacksmith shod him, and Jeff watched with interest. He couldn't see why the horse stood still and let Big Shorty hammer nails right into his hoofs. His own feet hurt just to watch it! But the big horse stood quietly.

"You're quite a hand with a horse," Big Shorty told Joe.

Joe's chest swelled. "I'm going to be a jockey when I grow up," he said. "I'm going to ride race-horses and win all the races."

"I thought you were going to Alaska and drive a dog sled," Jeff reminded him.

"Oh, I'll do that when I get too old to be a jockey," Joe said. "I'm going to live a long time."

"Jeff! Joe! Where are you?" Mrs. Kinnery's voice interrupted them.

Neither of the boys answered. They were having such a good time in the blacksmith's shop, and they knew that their mother was going to put them to work.

"Joe! Jeff! Answer me!" The call came again.

"Answer your ma!" Big Shorty told them.

"But she wants to put us to work."

"Answer her, anyway. When I was a kid I didn't do what my ma told me, and I got into all kinds of trouble. By the time I learned better, I didn't have any ma to tell me what to do. You answer her while you got the chance!"

30

Big Shorty looked so solemn that the boys were impressed. They trudged back to the cookhouse, wondering what kind of work awaited them. Mrs. Kinnery met them at the door with a big lunch basket, a gallon can full of coffee, and a large paper sack holding the things there was no room for anywhere else. "Take the lunch up to the men," she told them. "They're working right near the road, so you can't get lost."

Jeff and Joe looked at each other and grinned. They didn't mind *this* kind of work. They had just been waiting for a chance to explore the big woods.

3

THE BIG WOODS

WHEN Jeff and Joe had loaded themselves with all these things, Mrs. Kinnery gave them a pie pan neatly wrapped in waxed paper. "This is a chocolate pie for Uncle Boss," she told them. "Carry it carefully so you won't jar the meringue. There's nothing in the world Boss Kinnery likes as much as a chocolate pie, and this one ought to put him in a good humor."

Jeff and Joe started off, following the logging road into the big woods. As soon as they left the clearing they were in deep shade, where only a few splinters of sunlight found their way through the roof of pine needles. The air was warm, though, and their load was heavy.

"The first thing I'm going to do is make me a wagon,"

Joe said. "I can make a wagon easy as pie."

"Well, but you'd have to pull it. It would be just as hard as carrying things," Jeff objected.

"*I* wouldn't pull it!"

"Who would, then? I s'pose you're going to buy a horse?"

"You just wait and see."

There was little underbrush growing beneath the big pines. But along the edges of the road were thickets of service berries and buckbrush. Just ahead of the boys the twigs quivered; then suddenly something burst out of the bushes and cleared the road with a bound.

"What is it?" Jeff gasped.

"Deer! There's another. And another!"

At least ten deer bounded across the road, so fast that they seemed hardly to touch the ground. They did not run, but bounced like rubber balls. Looking after them, the boys could catch glimpses of them bouncing off in the distance between the straight yellow trunks of the pines.

The boys drew a deep breath. They had stopped stock-still in the road to watch. Now they decided to put down their heavy bundles and rest. They lay on their backs under a tree, looking up into the branches.

"There's something up there," Joe said. "I saw something move."

They waited, very still, and soon Jeff saw a tuft of

33

hair move down the trunk. It disappeared, then re-appeared closer to the ground. Again it disappeared. From the other side of the trunk a pointed nose, two pointed ears, and two bright black eyes thrust out. At last the whole animal ventured into sight, a tiny striped creature with a bushy tail as long as his body.

"It's a chipmunk! I wish we had something to feed it."

"That reminds me," Joe said, sitting up. "The men are waiting for their lunch. We'd better go on."

They picked up the basket, the sack, the coffee can, and the pie, and went on. They took turns carrying the pie, for they both wanted to please their uncle. "I ought to give it to him," Joe said. "I'm the oldest." He always reminded Jeff that he was older when he wanted to have something his way.

"No, I ought to give it to him," Jeff said. "I'm the one that spilled the coffee, so he's the maddest at me."

There was no denying that. "Well, maybe you'd better," Joe agreed.

"I wonder how much farther it is to where they're working? How will we know when we get there?"

"I don't know."

They looked around them. There was the road and there were the big trees. Somewhere, way up above the tallest trees, was the sky. But there was nothing to tell them where they were. "We'll just have to keep going," Joe said. "We're bound to get *somewhere*."

But as they stood there, they heard a sound. It was the steady rhythmic whine of a crosscut saw. "Whoosh-whoosh, whoosh-whoosh."

They knew they must be getting close, so they stepped along smartly. Soon they came to a turn-off from the road, and saw the marks of big wheels going off into the woods.

They could hear the saws clearly now, and farther away the sounds of axes and men's voices. From still farther away came a cracking noise, followed by a sighing; then a crash which echoed through the forest. A tree had come to earth.

Jeff and Joe went toward the sounds, stumbling over logs and around stumps, dodging through the brush, but managing to hold on to their burdens, including the precious pie. The stumps became more numerous and the trees farther apart. Now they could see the men up the hill sawing away at the big tree. The sawing stopped. One man removed the saw-handle, pulled the saw out, and, replacing the handle, put it carefully to one side. Meanwhile, the other man took up a sledge-hammer and pounded a wedge into the cut. Then both men stood back.

Jeff recognized Ole and Mac. He tried to attract their attention. They were not looking at the boys, however, but up into the top of the tree they had been sawing. "What are they looking at?" Jeff wondered.

Joe stopped and pointed. "Look! Look up there!"

Jeff followed his pointing finger. He saw the top of the tall tree sway gently and dip down as if it were bowing to them. It paused, then slowly, majestically, the giant pine began to fall straight toward them.

It seemed to fall for hours, and yet Jeff and Joe could not move from the spot. They just stood there, watching the boughs of the tree come closer and closer, as if reaching out for them. They saw it looming almost over their heads before they broke and ran down the hill. They dropped everything—lunch basket, coffee can, pie, and all. Sandwiches, apples, cookies, sugar jar, milk can—they flew in all directions.

A great wind seemed to be stirred up by the falling tree, and a *whishing* sound filled the air. Then came the crash. Twigs and pine cones, needles and broken limbs scattered and fell.

When the echoes died away, Jeff and Joe summoned up courage to look back. There was the topmost top of the tree a long way away. It had fallen far short of where they had been standing. They had not needed to run at all.

Jeff looked down at his feet. There lay the empty pie pan. For ten steps back the ground was spattered with chocolate pie. Little puffs of meringue decorated the bushes. He looked up, straight into the eyes of Boss Kinnery, who stood there, panting.

He was quite out of breath from running. He waved his arms and sputtered, but he was speechless. All he could do was point at the scattered sandwiches. Joe and Jeff began to gather them up. Sadly they retraced their steps, picking up the food as they went.

Ole and Mac came to help them. After everything they could find was collected, there was plenty for the men to eat. The coffee had not spilled, for the top of the can was screwed on tight, and the sandwiches were all right except for a few pine needles and ants.

"They just give an extra flavor," Mac told the boys. "Sit down here with us and take it easy."

"Nefer yu mind," Ole said kindly. "Dose pig trees,

dey always look like dey going to fall on yu. Dey fool anyboty."

Mac gave Jeff and Joe a sandwich apiece, and soon the boys began to feel better. They sat with Ole and Mac on a log out of sight of Uncle Boss. "You just stay out of his sight for a while," Mac advised. "Hey, Fred! Take these young apple-knockers with you before they get into any more trouble."

"Come on then," Fred told them. "I got to get back to work."

Jeff and Joe followed Fred. Now that the lunch basket was empty it was easy to carry. Behind them the saws began to whine.

"They've started cutting again," Jeff said.

"You don't cut a tree; you fall it!" Fred protested. "You kids got to learn how to talk. For instance, what would you say those men over there are doing?" He pointed to a group swinging their axes at the limbs of a fallen tree.

"I'd say they were chopping wood."

"Well, they ain't. They're limbing. There's all kinds of work in the woods. There's falling and bucking and limbing and swamping and bunching and—"

"What's bucking?" asked Jeff.

"What's swamping?" asked Joe.

"You just keep your eyes open as we go along. You see the limbers; they clean off the tree. Then the

39

swampers pile the limbs and brush into big piles."

"What for?"

"Because the Government says so. We are on Indian land, you know, and the Government tells us what to do."

"Indian land? Where are the Indians?" Jeff asked.

"Oh, all around on this side of the river." Fred waved his arm.

Joe wanted to know, "But *why* do you pile up the brush?"

"To keep from having forest fires."

"But what do you do with 'em?"

"We burn 'em."

"Then you have a fire anyway. Why—"

Fred growled, "I never heard so many questions in my life. Keep your eyes open, I tell you, and you'll learn more than by keeping your mouth open. See, there are the buckers at work. They saw the logs into sixteen-foot lengths. Then come the knot-knockers and the gophers."

Jeff had been trying to be quiet, but he just had to say, "I don't see any gophers."

"Little Shorty over there—he's a gopher. He digs the dirt out from under the log so's the buncher can get his line around it."

"The bunchers pile up the logs, I bet!" cried Joe. "I see 'em doing it."

40

They were walking as they talked, climbing over logs and around piles of boughs. The forest looked as if a storm had passed through, wrecking the magnificent trees. Only the smaller trees were left standing. The men scattered out among the wreckage, each man hard at work at his own job.

"Here's where I get to work myself," Fred said.

This was one of the busiest places of all. A clearing was filled with big horses, hitched in four-horse teams to pairs of enormous wheels. Fred swung himself up on the back of one of the horses. At a word from him the team pulled forward and the wheels lumbered off uphill. One by one, the other wheels followed.

The boys stood watching, and soon Fred came back, his wheels dragging a load of logs through the dust. He called to Jeff and Joe as he passed by. "See you later!"

They watched him ride out of sight. Other teams went cracking by, their loads scraping and swinging and breaking off brush as they went. The shouts of the men and the crack of their whips rang through the woods.

"Wonder where they're going?" said Jeff.

"Let's find out!" said Joe.

4

HER MAJESTY

"ALL RIGHT," Jeff said, "let's go." He started walking after the teams.

"I don't want to walk; I want to ride," said Joe.

Jeff looked at the heavy horses as they went by. Their big hoofs seemed to shake the earth. Their backs looked as wide as the logs themselves. "Do you think we could?"

"Sure we can. Hey, mister! Let us have a ride!" Joe called to the last driver who went by.

He was a fat man with a good-natured, whiskery face. "Well, why not?" he said, and pulled his horses to a stop. He pointed to the animal beside him. "If you can mount him, you can ride him."

The closer Jeff got to the horse, the taller it looked.

42

He thought it must be the tallest horse in the world. How would he ever get on its back? But Joe knew just what to do. He clambered around the big wheel and walked along the tongue which was fastened between the horses. He caught hold of the horse's harness and pulled himself onto its back. Jeff was not going to let himself be left behind. He followed Joe's lead, and the next thing he knew, he was sitting behind Joe on the horse's back. Joe held on to the hames which stood upright from the harness, and Jeff held on to Joe.

The fat man laughed. "Didn't think you could do it," he said. He cracked his whip and shouted to the team. With a heave the horses lurched forward. Jeff had a funny feeling in his stomach. His legs stuck out on each side of him and he bounced with every step. He wished he were back on the ground.

Joe sat up straight and thumped his legs against the horse's side. "This is the life! Beats walking, doesn't it?" he cried.

Jeff said, between bounces, "S-sure d-does." He thought longingly, however, of walking along the road on his own two feet. He would really have liked that better.

As soon as he got used to the motion, though, he began to enjoy it. The horse felt so warm and solid; and it *was* nice to be riding instead of walking. He looked around at the woods and wondered where they were

43

going. Where did the big wheels and the big logs go?

His question was answered when they came out of the pines at the bank of the river. The bank sloped steeply down to the water. At the edge the loads were released by the toggle-knockers, the wheels were pulled away, and the logs went tumbling into the river with a roar and a splash.

As Jeff and Joe rode up, they met Fred going back. His mouth fell open when he saw the boys. "What will you young'uns do next?" he exclaimed. "Get off there this minute! And stay off!"

"Awww!"

"That's the most dangerous thing you could do! What if you fell under the wheels? Or the horses' hoofs? Get 'em off of there, Chub."

"Better get off," the fat man told them.

Jeff and Joe slid down from their mount. Joe stuck out his underlip and scowled. "Nobody wants us to have any fun," he grumbled.

"Nobody wants you to get killed, either," Fred said as he drove off. "Do me a favor, will you, and see if you can't get home without getting into any more trouble?"

The boys sat on a stump for a while and watched the logs go thundering into the water. Sometimes they piled up into a tangle. When that happened, men would walk along the logs with pike-piles and push the jammed logs out into the current. They were called river-pigs. One of them almost got carried away on a log, but he leaped back to shore just in time. Jeff watched excitedly, but Joe was still sulking because his ride had been cut short.

"I'm going home," he said.

Jeff noticed then that the sun had already disappeared behind the tops of the trees. He remembered that they must still be a long way from camp.

One of the loaders showed them the way. If they walked down the river a little way, he said, they would come to a creek which ran into the river. Then, if they followed the creek, it would lead them back to Kinnery Camp.

The boys walked single file along the path and looked down on the river dashing by. It was as clear as glass where it ran deep, but became white as soapsuds where the rocks churned it into foam. Great logs went floating by on their way to the mill. Chips and twigs and splinters and chunks of bark bounced after them.

They came to the creek and turned toward camp. The roaring of the river died away in the distance,

46

and they heard the smaller voice of the creek rippling over the shadows. "It sounds like bells," Jeff said. "Hear it? Tinkle, Tinkle!"

"Those are real bells. Cowbells. See—there are the cows."

Ahead of them three cows had waded out into the creek. They dipped their muzzles into the water and raised them, dripping. They stared at Jeff and Joe.

"Boo! Shoo! Skat!" Joe shouted. He wanted to see them run.

"Don't you scare my cows!" a voice said.

Jeff and Joe looked for the speaker. Then they looked at each other. Where was he?

Joe scooped up some gravel and drew back his arm to throw it at the cows. Suddenly he felt a sharp blow on the seat of his pants. "Ouch!" He dropped the gravel.

"I told you not to scare my cows," said the voice.

The boys looked all around again. But they could not see a living creature other than the cows. Jeff thought he saw a movement in the bushes across the creek, but he wasn't sure. He didn't much like the idea of wading across to find out, with someone hiding and watching them.

The cows, startled by the loud voices, climbed out of the creek and made their way off on the other side. The boys looked after them. "Let's follow them and find out who it was," Joe said. "I'm not going to be scared off by any old voice!"

They took off their shoes and waded across. The water was icy. Their feet turned white, then red. They were glad to get their shoes and socks on again. The cows were out of sight in the brush, but they could follow them by the tinkling of their bells.

"Who do you s'pose it was?" Joe panted as they jogged up the hill.

"Maybe it was an echo," Jeff said hopefully.

"That wasn't any echo that whacked me in the pants," Joe said.

"Maybe it was an Indian. Fred said this was Indian land."

"It sounded like a kid to me. I'm not afraid of any kid!"

"I'm not afraid, either!" said Jeff. If Jeff did not seem to be as brave as Joe sometimes, it was because he had more imagination. While he stopped to imagine all the things that *could* happen, Joe plunged right ahead. The woods opened up and they could see the cows walking peacefully across a pasture toward an old farmhouse on the side of the hill. Still there was no one in sight.

They stopped at the edge of the woods. The ruddiness of the light told them that the sun was setting behind the mountains. "We'd better go back. I'm hungry," Joe said, but as he turned he felt another stinging blow on the same tender spot. He whirled, his red hair bristling just like Uncle Boss's. This time he saw the bushes shake. He plowed right into the middle of them.

Jeff dived in after him. For a minute he thought that the bushes themselves were alive, for the limbs were whipping around and his mouth and ears were full of leaves. Somebody was kicking and scratching. "Ouch!" cried Joe. "I think I've got hold of a wildcat!"

He pulled his captive out where he could see. When Jeff could get the leaves out of his eyes he stared in surprise. Joe had captured, not a wildcat, but a girl. She was smaller than Jeff. She had coppery skin, large black eyes, and a mane of straight black hair. She wore a pink dress, and she stuck out a very pink tongue at Joe and Jeff.

"Where is he?" Joe demanded.

"Where's who?"

"Whoever it was that threw a rock at me."

The girl smiled sweetly. She held up a slingshot in one hand, and showed him a handful of pebbles in the other.

Joe was disgusted. To think that he had gone to all that trouble just to catch a little Indian girl! "Come on, Jeff!" he said.

But Jeff wanted to know more about the girl. He liked the way she looked—and he admired the way she

had fought. "Who are you?" he asked.

"Who are you?" she countered.

"I'll tell you my name if you'll tell me yours."

"All right. Her Majesty Queen Victoria."

Jeff gasped.

"They call me Maggie for short."

Joe called, "Are you going to stay here all night?" He was halfway down to the creek. "Come on!"

Jeff said quickly, "My name is Jeff. I live at Kinnery Camp. Do you live over there?" He pointed to the farmhouse.

She nodded.

"I'll come to see you if you want me to," Jeff offered.

She nodded again.

"Good-by."

She waved her hand. Jeff started off, but he came back. "I'm sorry we scared your cows," he told Maggie. "What kind of a name is Her Majesty Queen Victoria, anyway?"

"It's the name of a queen. My daddy went all the way to England when he was in school, and played baseball before the queen herself. He named me for her."

"I was named for two presidents," Jeff bragged. "My father named me for Thomas Jefferson and my mother named me for Jefferson Davis. So my name is really Thomas Jefferson Davis Kinnery, but they call me

51

Jeff. Do you bring the cows to the creek every night?"

She nodded. She never seemed to use words if she could do without them.

"Good-by."

Again she waved her hand, and this time she smiled.

Jeff ran down the hill and splashed across the creek. He was very hungry, but he felt good. He had learned so many new things that day, and he had made a new friend.

5

THE CONTRAPTION

JEFF AND JOE sometimes agreed with Uncle Boss that a logging camp was no place for kids. Every morning they were roused from their beds at five o'clock. They helped with breakfast; they served the cackleberries, liver pads, skid-grease and java; they washed dishes and peeled potatoes. Above all, they peeled potatoes! Big Shorty was right; they were never through peeling potatoes.

But in spite of all the work they had to do, they found time to enjoy themselves, too. Joe was building a wagon. He could be found most any day at the blacksmith's shop, hammering away at his wagon or helping Big Shorty with the horses. Jeff often joined them there, for he loved to watch the sparks fly from Big Shorty's hammer, and to see the metal take shape on the anvil.

When Joe's wagon was finished, Jeff said, "Let's play with it. We can take turns pushing each other."

"No, sir," Joe answered. "I'm not going to push any wagon."

"Well, what did you make it for, then?" asked Jeff, disappointed.

"You just wait and see." Joe loved to tell Jeff that, acting very grown up, and Jeff did not like it at all.

So the wagon was left at the back door of the cookhouse, outside the room where Joe and Jeff slept. Joe wouldn't let anyone touch it. But he wouldn't play with it, either. Jeff thought he was mean.

One day when Jeff and Joe were at the blacksmith's shed, an old hound came to the door and looked in. "Hello!" said Joe. "Where did you come from?"

"Nobody knows where them dogs come from," Big Shorty said. "They drift into camp ever so often. Mostly they're Indian dogs, come over here for a square meal."

Joe patted the hound on his wrinkled forehead and pulled his long drooping ears. "I think I'll name you Jasper."

"No use to name him. They hang around camp a while, but they always go away again," Big Shorty told him.

"Jasper won't go away. Come on, Jasper. Let's get something to eat." Joe went off to the cookhouse, followed by the hound, who waved his tail gratefully.

Jeff stayed to finish twisting a piece of wire he had found. He was interrupted by his mother's calling him to come take the lunches to the men. As he walked toward the cookhouse he met Joe coming down the road. He was leading Jasper. And Jasper was hitched to the wagon. The wagon was loaded with lunches. Jasper was a big dog, and he pulled the wagon easily. He looked as if he wanted to look happy about his new job, but his natural expression was so sad that he just couldn't.

Jeff cried, "Oh, good! Jasper will carry the lunches instead of us!"

"I'll have to lead him a while," Joe said, "but it won't be long before I can just walk along beside him and say *Gee* and *Haw*."

Jasper wagged his tail as if he knew what the words meant already. He pulled the wagon all the way to the place where the men were working, but on the way back Jeff tried to get a ride in the wagon, and Jasper wouldn't pull. "You're too heavy," Joe told him. "You just wait until another dog comes around camp. I'll have me a dog team before I'm through, and then we can both ride."

They had fun with Jasper and the wagon all day, and that night Jasper slept on the floor beside their bed. Jeff and Joe slept in a storeroom at the back of

55

the cookhouse. The walls were covered with shelves loaded with canned goods, boxes of dried apples and prunes, jars of pickles and preserves, and all kinds of supplies.

Jeff had a bad habit of getting hungry as soon as he went to bed. Sometimes he solved this problem by eating a handful of dried apples, followed by a dipper full of water. The dried apples would swell up inside of him, and, feeling comfortably full, he would go to sleep. But once in a while he ate too *many* apples, or drank too *much* water. Then he felt as if his stomach would pop like a balloon. This was one of those nights.

Jeff lay awake long after Joe and Jasper had gone to sleep. He was too uncomfortable to sleep, but not uncomfortable enough to call his mother. He knew how much she needed her rest after working hard all day. He lay and listened to the sounds of the night. He could hear the wind sighing through the tops of the pines, and the faint tinkle of the stream at the bottom of the hill. He heard an owl somewhere in the big woods. He heard some Indian dogs barking at the farm where Maggie lived. Now and then he heard voices from the bunkhouses, and knew that some of the men were still awake.

All of these sounds Jeff recognized, but there was another sound underneath all the others which he did not recognize. At first he thought it might be the squealing of pigs. But there was a sort of tune to the squealing. Pigs could not sing! No, Jeff decided, it was some kind of music. But what kind? And who was making it? He just had to go and find out.

As Jeff climbed out of bed, Joe woke up. "Where are you going?" he demanded.

"I'm going to find out about the music."

"What music?"

"Listen!" said Jeff.

They listened. Jasper woke up and listened, too. The music seemed to come close, then to go farther away. It was the strangest kind of music they had ever heard.

Joe climbed out of bed, too. "I'll go with you."

They pulled on their trousers and their shoes and slipped out of the back door. Jasper padded along beside them. It was very dark all around, but the sky above the clearing was powdered with millions of brilliant stars. When Jeff, Joe, and Jasper came around the cookhouse they could see the lamps lighting up in the bunkhouses, one by one. Men came out of the tents in their long underwear and looked up and down the road.

"What is that blasted noise?"

"Where is it?"

"I thought it was Big Shorty snoring."

"It's music."

"Do you call *that* music?"

The men were shouting back and forth from one bunkhouse to the other. They peered up and down the road.

As they watched, they saw a man marching up the road toward them. He was holding a peculiar looking thing. And it was from this thing that the music came. He marched straight up to the group. It was Mac. He was holding a bag with pipes sticking out from it, and blowing into a mouthpiece. The music came out of the pipes. When he reached the men he stopped playing. "What's all the fuss about?" he asked.

The men broke into a clamor. "What's all the fuss

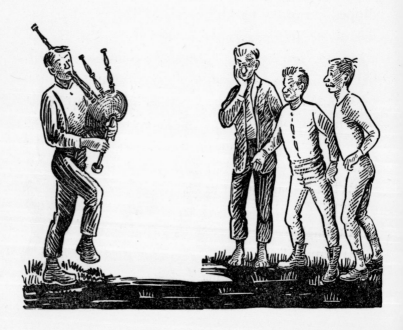

about, he says!"

"I thought it was hog-killing time!"

"When are we supposed to get some sleep?"

"What is that animal you're carrying, Mac? Can't you put it out of its misery?"

Mac looked surprised. "Didn't you ever hear of bagpipes? I ordered them from a mail-order house, and this is the first chance I've had to try them out."

Jeff remembered the mysterious black box they had brought with them in the wagon. Now he knew what was in it.

"Try them out in the daytime, why don't you?" Fred

protested. "They might even sound good then."

"I work in the daytime."

Ole wanted to know, "Vot kind of contraption yu got dere, Mac?"

Mac showed them the instrument. Now that the breath was out of it, it had collapsed like an empty paper bag. The men crowded around to look at it. "How'd you learn to play the thing?" Chub asked.

"My father taught me. He was a piper in Scotland, and all his ancestors were, too. He had to sell his pipes after he came to this country, but I always said when I had enough money saved up I'd buy me some." He stroked the bagpipes proudly. He put the mouthpiece to his lips.

"Now look here," one of the men said, "I got as much respect for ancestors as anybody, but I need my sleep. Lay off of that."

Mac looked at the men. "Yeah, that's right," Big Shorty said. "Music's music, and sleep's sleep. They don't mix."

"But—" Mac was getting angry. "I have a right to play if I want to."

"Not in front of *my* bunkhouse," Big Shorty said. He was getting angry, too.

Mac looked for a safe place to put down his bagpipes. Seeing a stump nearby, he carefully dusted off the top and placed the pipes upon it. Then he took off his heavy wool shirt and pushed up his undershirt sleeves. "Come on," he said to Big Shorty, "Come on! We'll settle this right now."

Big Shorty seemed to swell to twice his size. He didn't have to take off his shirt, for he had nothing on but his red flannel union suit. He pushed up his sleeves. "All right, if that's the way you want it!" He began dancing around Mac with his fists clenched.

Some of the men tried to stop them. "Aw, go to bed and cool off!" Chub begged. But others egged Mac and Big Shorty on. "Bring a lamp," Little Shorty cried. Jeff, Joe, and Jasper waited to see what would happen next.

Suddenly a deep voice interrupted. There stood Boss Kinnery, his red hair standing on end. "What's going on here?" he roared. "If you want to stay up all night and sleep tomorrow, it's all right with me, but I'm not going to pay you for doing it! Break it up!"

He stepped between Mac and Big Shorty, holding them apart at arm's length. "Hit your bunks, everybody. *I'll* settle this."

The men retreated into their bunkhouses, and went grumbling to bed. Boss Kinnery heard what Mac and Big Shorty had to say. When they had finished, he said, "Now, you know you can't work up a real good temper over that! Pick up your contraption, Mac, and make 'er squeal."

Mac puffed and wheezed. The music began to wail. "Now, walk down the road." Mac marched off, the music growing fainter and fainter. "Now," Boss said to Big Shorty, "speak up when it gets far enough away so it won't disturb your beauty sleep."

"I guess it wouldn't bother me now," Big Shorty admitted.

"All right!" Boss Kinnery called out to Mac. "Put a mark on that tree. Then play till you bust, if you want to, but don't come any closer!"

Big Shorty went to bed, Mac marched off into the darkness. Boss Kinnery turned to go back to his own bunk in his room at the cookhouse. Then he noticed Jeff, Joe, and Jasper, still standing there. "I might have known you kids would be right in the middle of this!" he growled. "Go to bed. If anyone wakes me up again tonight, I'll forget I'm a peace-loving man."

6

THE HUCKLEBERRY PATCH

WHEN MRS. KINNERY heard about the little Indian girl and her cows, she lost no time in arranging
to buy fresh milk for Kinnery Camp. Maggie's father,
Chief John, was an old friend of Boss Kinnery's. He
was willing to sell him any extra milk he had, and
eggs as well. The arrangement improved the meals at
the camp, but it also added another job to those the
boys already had. Every evening they took a bucket and
a basket to the farm, and Jasper pulled the supplies
back in the wagon.

Joe had his hands full on these trips, because every
dog at the farm—and there were at least a dozen of
them—came out to chase Jasper away. They followed,
barking, until Jasper was safely on the other side of the

63

creek. They did not dare cross into his territory. Jeff and Joe put stepping-stones in the creek for themselves, but Jasper had to wade, and once across the creek he would shake himself vigorously. Joe could not break him of this habit, but just had to hold on to the milk bucket and the egg basket and hope for the best.

Jeff would have liked to stay and play with Maggie, but Joe wasn't the least bit interested. As for Maggie, she never failed to put out her tongue at Joe. He could see her slingshot sticking out of her pocket, and it always made him mad.

One afternoon when Joe was training Jasper to a new harness, Jeff decided to keep his promise and visit Maggie at the farm. As he came near, the dogs rushed out as usual, barking. Maggie came out on the porch and waved to Jeff. She waded out through the dogs to meet him. She had a basket in her hand.

"I'm going to pick huckleberries," she said. "Want to go?"

"Sure I do!" said Jeff.

The pasture sloped upward from the house, rising steeper and steeper. Groves of trees and patches of brush took the place of open pasture as they climbed. They followed a well-worn path which led over the top of the hill.

Behind that hill rose another, and behind that one the great rough slopes at the foot of Snow Mountain began. Behind Snow Mountain a whole range of mountains loomed, but Snow Mountain rose so high that its snow-covered peak hid all the others from sight.

Jeff had never come this way before. It was fun to be so high that he could look down on the camp. He could see the clearing and the tents and the cookhouse with the blue smoke coming out of the chimney. He could see the broken places in the forest where the lumberjacks were working. It was fun to look down on the tops of those tall, tall trees!

"Come on," called Maggie. She was up above him on the trail, for she had been climbing while he was looking around. He had to run to catch up.

"Where does the trail go?" Jeff asked. "Does it go to the top of the mountain?"

She shook her head.

"Isn't there any trail to the top of the mountain?"

"Why should anybody go up there?" she asked.

"Well, just to get to the top."

"Why?"

Jeff could not answer her, though it seemed reason enough to him. "Don't you ever wonder what's up there?" he asked.

Maggie looked surprised. "No, I never did. But now I do. Let's ask my daddy. He knows everything."

They had come to thickets of huckleberry bushes, and Jeff saw people scattered here and there over the mountainside, picking the berries. Maggie took him to where Chief John, a big man in a red shirt, was working. "What's on top of the mountain, Daddy?" she asked.

Chief John smiled at Jeff, but frowned at their empty basket. "When you fill your basket, I'll answer your question," he said.

Jeff and Maggie went to work. It was not really *work*, Jeff thought. There were lots of berries, and all they had to do was pick them and drop them into the basket. Now and then he popped one into his mouth. It was much nicer than peeling potatoes.

Sometimes they came close to other people at work. Maggie's mother was there, and her three sisters and her grown-up brother and his wife, and her baby brother riding on her mother's back. They all talked together in their own language, and laughed at one another's jokes. Jeff wished that he could understand what they were saying, so that he could laugh, too.

As the pickers filled their baskets they gathered around some blankets spread on the ground beside a fire. Maggie's mother put the baby on a blanket, and one by one the family sat down to rest and warm their hands. It was growing chilly. Jeff and Maggie were the last to fill their basket, since they had come late.

When they carried their load to the fire, Chief John motioned for them to sit down beside him. "What is this question about the top of the mountain?" he asked.

"We want to know what's up there, Daddy."

Chief John turned and looked up toward the mountaintop, which still held the light of the setting sun. "You can see for yourself what's up there," he said. "Snow."

"Isn't there anything else but snow?" Jeff asked.

Chief John had a faraway look in his eyes. "Below the snow line there are many beautiful flowers. Farther down there are little scrubby trees, and then there are the big trees." He paused. "Among the big trees there is a lake."

"What is the name of the lake?"

"It is called Lost Valley Lake."

"Why?"

Chief John laughed. "When our people learned to speak English they learned one word too many. It is like a mosquito, and our children use it to bite us with. Why! Why! Why!" he teased.

"But why *is* it called Lost Valley Lake, Daddy?" Maggie giggled.

Her father grew serious. "For a very good reason," he said. "It was once not a lake at all, but a little valley. It was too high on the mountain for a dwelling place, but every year the people went there for the fall hunting, to kill meat for the winter. They camped in brush houses under the big trees on the bank of a stream."

67

Jeff could tell from the sound of Chief John's voice that he had forgotten about him and Maggie and the others and was thinking about things that had happened long ago. Jeff stared at the mountain, and as Chief John talked, he, too, forgot about the huckleberry patch and imagined that he was in the lost valley.

"Every year they went there," Chief John went on. "Every year the smoke rose from the fires, drying the meat, fish, and berries for the winter to come. Everyone was busy, but everyone was joyful, too. It was said that in ancient times the people had lived in caves in the side of the mountain, and that the spirits of their ancestors dwelt there still. It was a place sacred to the tribe.

"The hunting was always good there, and the people never went hungry. There were flocks of ducks and geese in the tules, fish in the stream, deer in the woods, rabbits in the thickets, and bear in the rocky heights. The people thought it would always be that way.

"Then, one year, the people came and raised their huts as usual. They built their fires and sent out their hunting parties. They set their fish traps, their bird snares, and made ready for the feasting and the plenty. The drying racks were soon loaded. The people danced and sang far into the night.

"But when they awoke one morning, the valley was very quiet. No bird sang; no squirrel chattered; not even the leaping of a fish broke the silence.

"They asked themselves what could be the meaning of this silence. Their chief pointed to the sky far above them. There they saw a wavering arrow pointing south. It was the geese flying high overhead. 'It is a sign,' the chief said. 'All living things have left the valley. We, too, must go.'

"But the people said, 'Why should we be frightened away from our valley of plenty? The creatures are only in hiding, perhaps from an approaching storm. We have only to wait, and all will be well again.'

"So they did not obey the chief, but spent the morning gaming and feasting. At noon a rumbling sound echoed from the mountain. 'Hear?' the people said. 'It is the thunder. There will be a storm, but we are protected deep in the valley, and when it is over all will be as usual.' But the chief rose and said, 'I and my family shall leave the valley. Who goes with us?' The people refused, and the chief took his family and began to climb out of the valley.

"The path was steep. The chief would not stop to rest, however, but led his wives and children upward until they stood on the ridge above. Then they looked back. As they watched, the side of the mountain opened up with a roar, and a river of fire poured out. Ashes filled the air and rocks flew about their heads. The stream of fire spilled over into the valley, damming up the river and raising clouds of steam. Mingled with the smoke of burning trees, they saw the smoke of the camp still rising, but they knew that they would never see their people again. As the fire came closer, they ran for their lives down the mountain."

Chief John stopped talking, as if that were the end of the story. But Jeff wanted to know more. "Did the chief ever go back?"

"No," Chief John shook his head. "He never went back. But his son went back once, when he was an old man. He could not find the valley at all. He found only a lake, a very clear, deep lake. Climbing upon an overhanging rock, he looked down upon the branches of tall trees, still standing there under the water. They

were white and bare, like giant bones. He went away quickly."

"Did *he* ever go back?"

"No, no one has been there since." Chief John stood up. His son kicked out the fire, carefully smothering the flames. "It is late," he said to Jeff. "They will wonder at the camp why you are not home yet."

"I'd better run!" Jeff said. "Mama will be worried. And Uncle Boss will be mad."

Maggie thrust the berry basket into his hands. "Take him some berries."

"Thanks!" Jeff bounded off down the trail. "Thanks for the berries! Thanks for the story! Good-by!" It was so easy to run downhill that he was almost out of sight before he could finish his speech.

He ran a race with the darkness. Down the mountain, down the hill, across the pasture, through the woods, across the creek, and up the path he ran. The men were already eating in the cookhouse, and as he came up the steps he saw his uncle waiting at the door.

"What do you mean by staying out so late?" Boss Kinnery demanded. "Your mother's been worried to death. She burned the stew."

Jeff tried to catch his breath. "I'm sorry, Uncle Boss," he panted. "We had to pick a whole basket full before Chief John would answer our question, and to

72

answer the question he had to tell a long story, and I forgot about supper."

"What? Talk sense!" Uncle Boss thundered.

Jeff held up his basket. "Please don't be mad, Uncle Boss. I brought you some berries. Maggie and I picked them ourselves."

Boss Kinnery just looked at them.

"Eat one, Uncle Boss. They're awful good."

His uncle hesitated, then took a berry and put it in his mouth. "Umm," he said, and took another. "Umm humm," he said, and took a handful. "It's been a long time since I picked huckleberries."

"Did you use to pick huckleberries, too, Uncle Boss?" Jeff asked.

"Oh, I was a champion picker in the old days. I remember one summer, when your pa and I were courting the same girl, we used to see who could fill her basket the quickest."

Jeff was surprised. He was surprised that Uncle Boss should take time to talk to him at all. And he was extra surprised to think that Uncle Boss had ever courted a girl. But Jeff was seldom so surprised that he could not ask questions. "Which one of you *did* fill her basket first?" he asked.

Uncle Boss wore a funny expression. His eyebrows came down as if he wanted to frown, but one corner of his mouth went up as if he wanted to smile. "*I did,*"

73

he said, "but while I was busy picking huckleberries, your pa proposed to the girl. So she married him instead of me."

Jeff was puzzled. "But—"

Uncle Boss interrupted him. "The Indians are having a festival at the Agency next week, to celebrate the huckleberry crop. They have one every year. How would you like to go?"

"Oh, I'd *like* to go, Uncle Boss!"

"Well, then, ask your mother if she'd like to go, too."

7

THE HUCKLEBERRY FESTIVAL

NEXT WEEK seemed a long time coming. But finally the day came, and Jeff, Joe, Mrs. Kinnery, and Uncle Boss started off to the Agency where the Indians were gathered. Jasper wanted to go with them in the wagon, but Uncle Boss shoved him out. "We've got enough of a menagerie as it is!" he said.

"Now look here, Boss Kinnery!" Mrs. Kinnery flared. "If you can't talk nice about the boys—"

"All right, all right, Polly," Uncle Boss hastened to pacify her. "This is a holiday. Kids are all right on holidays. I still say that a logging camp is no place for kids, but I'm willing to drop the argument for the day."

Uncle Boss drove the horses. Mrs. Kinnery sat beside him on the front seat, and Jeff and Joe sat in chairs in the back. Looking back, Joe saw that Jasper was following, his tongue and his long ears flopping. He did not say anything about it, however, and neither did Jeff. They both thought Jasper ought to have a holiday too.

There were other wagons on the road, and several Indians came by on horseback and on foot. Boss Kinnery spoke to all of them. He seemed to know everybody, and everybody seemed to be going to the celebration.

Not far from the Agency the crowd was so thick that Uncle Boss decided to leave the wagon. He hitched the horses under some trees. "We'll come back to the wagon at noon and have our lunch," Mrs. Kinnery said. "We have time to do some shopping at the store before then."

Jeff and Joe did not want to spend their time in a store. They could see the Indians' camps scattered through the woods. "Can we go over to the campground?" they asked. Jeff added, "Maybe we will find Maggie and Chief John."

Their mother hesitated, but Uncle Boss said, "Sure, go ahead. Just be sure you know your way back to the wagon."

"And be sure you get back here for your lunch!" Mrs. Kinnery said.

Jeff and Joe found Jasper waiting for them by the side of the road. He wagged his tail and started off to the campground as if he knew the way well. Jeff and Joe followed him.

The Indians had set up their camps here and there under the trees surrounding the Agency. Some of them had pitched tents, some had built brush houses like those their ancestors lived in before the white men came, and some had no shelter but the branches of the trees. There was a public well near the Agency buildings, and a clear mountain stream wandered through the woods, furnishing plenty of water. Little fires smouldered at each camping place, and there was so much cooking, so much coming and going for water, so much visiting from fire to fire, and so much general moving about that it seemed like one great big party.

It was cool under the trees, and wherever a clearing let the sun through, a group of Indians gathered to enjoy its warmth. Jeff, Joe, and Jasper stumbled almost into the middle of such a group before they could stop. A dozen or more men were sitting in two rows facing each other. One very old man, wrapped in a blanket, was singing. The others followed his lead, swaying from side to side in time to the music. As they sang, the old man held up two small bones. One was marked with black lines, while the other was plain. Then, still singing, he changed the bones back and forth from one hand to the other. He did it so fast, and with so many jerks and gestures, that Jeff and Joe soon lost track of

where they were. The old man's face was blank.

"It's a game," Joe whispered to Jeff. "One side hides the bones, and the other side guesses where they are."

Sure enough, after a few moments the singing stopped and a man on the opposite side pointed to one of the old man's hands. All the players were tense and silent. They almost held their breaths with excitement. The old man opened his hands and a cry went up. The player had guessed wrong. The loser gave the winner a stick, which the old man added to a pile by his side.

"That must be the way they keep score. Look; the old man's side has more sticks than the other. They have won."

The old man caught sight of Jeff and Joe. He smiled at them. His smile was just one more wrinkle among all the other wrinkles in his face. He spoke to them in the Indian language. Of course the boys did not understand what he said, but they understood that he was friendly. While the players were resting from the game, the old man showed Jeff and Joe the bones. They were polished and yellow with age. A younger man explained to the boys how the game was played. He moved the bones so skillfully that Jeff blinked his eyes trying to follow their movements. They tried guessing which hand the plain bone was in, but they failed every time. "The plain bone is called 'the Woman,' the young man said. "The one with the lines scratched on it is called 'the Man.' The game is to find 'the Woman.' But she is like all women—she likes to deceive. These are very old bones. They have always been in this man's family." The old man nodded, smiling at the boys.

The game began again. The players began to sing. Jeff and Joe grew sleepy, listening to the deep voices and watching the flying hands. Jasper trotted away, and the boys followed him.

They soon waked up. There were so many things to see! There was a baseball game going on in a meadow, and a meeting being held in a small church building. Everything seemed to be going on at once. People went from one gathering to another. In the clearing outside the church a crowd was clustered around something the boys could not see. Of course they wanted to find out what was happening. They squeezed through the circle and found themselves watching an extraordinary sight.

A fat Indian woman in a red print dress was jigging up and down. As she danced, she took a stalk from a bundle of tules beside her and dipped it into a can of kerosene. Still jigging up and down, she lighted a match and set the tule on fire. Then she put it in her mouth! For a moment the boys thought she had swallowed it, but no, she brought it out again, the fire gone.

"She's eating fire!" Jeff cried.

"That reminds me, it must be time to eat," Joe said. "But I'm not *that* hungry!"

They squeezed out of the crowd and ran back to the wagon. Their mother and Uncle Boss were there, laying out the lunch. It looked very good.

"Come and get it, boys," Mrs. Kinnery called.

Jeff fell to at once, but Joe dragged out the horses' nosebags and put them on the patient team. Each horse nodded and nuzzled him gratefully. Then Joe sat down to eat, but every time he took a bite he held another behind him over the edge of the wagon. He knew that Jasper was waiting underneath, ready to catch whatever was dropped to him.

Uncle Boss demanded, "What are you doing with your food? It's not so easy to get that we can afford to throw it away. What's under the wagon there?"

"Jasper's there."

"You've thrown enough food overboard to feed *three* Jaspers," Uncle Boss grumbled. He leaned over and looked under the wagon. Sure enough, Jasper was there, but there were also two other dogs. One was a small slick tan dog with black spots. The other was large and white and shaggy. All of them were hungry.

Boss Kinnery waved his arms. "You'll never get rid of 'em if you feed 'em! They'll follow you back to camp. Shoo! Skat!"

Joe said, "The big shaggy one will make a good team-mate for Jasper at the wagon. I'm going to call him Husky, because he looks like one. I'll bet the little terrier will hunt rats. Toby is a good name for him."

His uncle opened his mouth to say something, but Mrs. Kinnery spoke first. "Remember, Boss; this is a holiday!"

Boss swallowed. Mrs. Kinnery smiled. Jeff and Joe and the three dogs went on eating. They were enjoying the huckleberry festival.

In the afternoon there were contests among the Indian men and boys—foot races, broad jumps, high jumps, and hop-skip-and-jumps. Then came the horse races.

Everyone lined up on one side of the road or the other. Some went a quarter of a mile up the road where the horses were to start, but most gathered at the

81

Agency store where the finish line was drawn. Joe saw Chief John leading a horse toward the starting place, and he ran to catch up with him. Maggie was following her daddy as usual, but when she saw Jeff she went with him instead to find a spot in front where she could see the race. "Is that Chief John's horse?" Jeff asked.

"Yes. His name is Home Run. He's the fastest horse on the Reservation."

"Does he always win?"

"No, but he is the fastest, anyway."

"Then why doesn't he win?"

"My daddy is too heavy to ride him any more. Lately my brother rides him in the races, but he is a big man, too. They tried to teach my cousin how, but Daddy says he hasn't got as much sense as the horse. I wish they'd let me ride. But they won't, 'cause I'm a girl." This was a very long speech for Maggie.

A pistol was fired. Every head in the crowd turned to look up the road. Almost at once a cloud of dust could be seen, and the horses came pounding into view.

"There he is—in second place. Come on, Home Run! Come on!"

Maggie's brother was riding Home Run. Jeff started screaming, "Come on, Home Run!" as loudly as he could. Every person in the crowd was calling out the name of his favorite. A big black horse was in the lead. A small, slender Indian boy was riding him, lying

82

almost flat on his neck. Home Run was trying his best to catch up, but he was carrying a much heavier load. Maggie's brother rode bareback to make himself as light as possible, but he was a big, heavy young man. Home Run strained every muscle to reach the black horse. Inch by inch he gained on him.

"He's even with him!" Jeff cried.

"He's passing him!"

"He's over the finish line. He's won! He's won!" Jeff jumped up and down.

Maggie explained. "No, he hasn't won yet. There are so many horses and the road is so narrow that they have to have three or four races. Then the winners have a run-off race. Home Run will have to win that, too."

As each race was run the excitement grew higher. There were four races in all, and then the four winners were led off to line up for the run-off race. "If only Home Run had a smaller rider!" sighed Maggie. "He could win over all of them—I know he could!"

"Bang!" went the starting signal. "Here they come!" the crowd yelled.

"Where's Home Run? There he is! But who is that riding him?"

Jeff almost choked with surprise. "It's Joe!"

Sure enough, there came Home Run, leading all the other horses, and there was Joe clinging to his back for dear life. They galloped headlong down the home stretch. Home Run was almost a length ahead. In another moment he would be across the finish line.

Suddenly Home Run shied at something. Joe gripped him with his knees, but the horse swerved so violently that he lost his balance. Home Run reared on his hind legs. Over went Joe, arms and legs waving as if he were trying to fly. He fell sprawling on the ground while people came running from all directions. Home Run trotted on to the finish line. But he had lost the race.

Joe was carried to the wagon. Jeff, Maggie, Mrs. Kinnery, and Uncle Boss gathered around. Chief John and his son came as quickly as they could. Jasper, Toby, and Husky jumped around the wagon and whined.

"I'm all right," said Joe. He moved his arms and legs to show that he wasn't hurt. "Go away and leave me alone!" He was trying not to cry.

Mrs. Kinnery made sure he had not broken any bones. "He's all right," she said. "There's nothing wrong with him but temper."

"Well, he can sulk all the way home," Uncle Boss said. "Let's go." He was in a temper, too.

Chief John said, "The boy is a good rider. It was my fault for not taking time to saddle the horse. Better luck next time!"

Jeff called good-by to Maggie and her family. He didn't want to leave the celebration. He could hear singing at the church, and caught a glimpse of the Indians dancing as they drove by.

Joe sulked and Uncle Boss argued all the way home. "This ought to prove to you that this is no place for kids!" Uncle Boss kept saying to Mrs. Kinnery. "They can't stay out of trouble for two minutes! Give them an inch and they'll take a mile. Aren't you ready to send 'em back to town, now, Polly?"

"No," said Mrs. Kinnery.

"What if your young bareback rider had broken a leg? Or his neck? You have to admit he'd be better off in town. Come on, admit it!"

"No."

Boss Kinnery waved his arms. The team thought he was slapping the reins on their backs on purpose, and broke into a trot. "Now look," Boss said. "Summer's over. It's nearly time for the boys to go to school. What are you going to do about that?"

Mrs. Kinnery lifted her chin. "There's a school at Battle Creek."

86

"But it's four miles from camp! You needn't think I'm going to drive 'em back and forth in the wagon."

"They can walk."

Jeff and Joe listened. All the pleasure of the Huckleberry Festival was gone. Joe knew that the lumberjacks would hear of his falling off the horse and that they would never let him forget it. His lower lip stuck out farther and farther as they got nearer to Kinnery Camp. It did not cheer him up to learn that he would have to walk four miles to school. Jeff did not feel cheerful, either. He didn't want to walk to school. He didn't want to go to school at all.

8

SCHOOL

As THE MORNINGS grew colder and colder, it grew harder and harder for Jeff and Joe to get up out of their warm bed. One morning there was ice on the water barrel when they went to get the water. That was the morning that they were to start to school.

They had peeled the potatoes the night before, but they had to set the table and serve the breakfast and clear away the dishes as usual. While they pulled on their jackets and laced up their boots, their mother told them once more just how to get to the schoolhouse at Battle Creek.

All the men had gone to work except Boss Kinnery and Big Shorty, who still sat by the stove. It was a gray, cloudy day outside, with a raw wind. Nobody seemed

88

to feel very cheerful. The boys looked as gloomy as they felt.

"You look like you're going to a funeral," Big Shorty teased them. "Cheer up! It won't hurt you to get some learning."

Boss Kinnery growled, "They ought to be back in town."

Mrs. Kinnery paid no attention to him. "Now run along, boys." She patted them on their shoulders and gave them their lunch boxes. "Don't be late to school. Be polite to your teacher. And start home the minute school is out."

"All right, Mamma," the boys answered, but they did not go. They hated to leave the warm room. Jasper and the other dogs lay behind the stove. It didn't seem fair that they could stay and be comfortable when Jeff and Joe could not.

"Well, what are you waiting for? A horse and buggy?" their uncle demanded.

"A race-horse, maybe!" Big Shorty laughed.

Joe slammed out of the house. He was tired of being teased about the race he had lost by being thrown off Chief John's horse. The men loved to tease him just to see him stick out his lower lip and scowl. Jeff followed Joe, and together they trudged off down the road.

Mrs. Kinnery went to the door and looked after

them. "They look mighty small under the big trees," she said.

Boss Kinnery came to the door, too, and looked out. "You ought to have better sense than to let them walk that far," he grumbled.

Jeff and Joe were nearly out of sight. Suddenly Boss opened the door and roared after them. "Hey there! Come back here!" Then he said to Big Shorty, "You've got some kind of a horse in the corral, haven't you? Saddle up whatever you can spare."

When Jeff and Joe came puffing back they found Big Shorty leading a tall, bony, brown horse up to the steps. "You'll have to get on the steps to mount him," he explained. "Jeff, you get up behind. Now, Joe, if you run this horse, I'll skin you alive."

Mrs. Kinnery looked doubtful. "I'd rather have them walk to school than ride a dangerous horse. Is he dangerous?"

"No, ma'am, but he likes to run. His grandmother had a relative that was first cousin to a thoroughbred."

"You'll be careful, won't you, Joe?"

"Sure I will, Mamma!" Joe was smiling like the noonday sun at the idea of having a horse to ride.

He clucked to the horse and they jogged away. Jeff bounced behind the saddle, waving good-by. Mrs. Kinnery turned. "Thank you, Boss," she said. But Uncle Boss had gone.

90

On the way to Battle Creek Jeff and Joe met Maggie. She and two other girls were riding a patient old farm-horse with a long, easy walk like a rocking chair. Maggie stuck out her tongue at Joe and smiled at Jeff. Joe tried to ignore the girls, but it was hard to pretend that all three of them weren't there. He kept up his dignified silence, though, while Jeff chattered and the girls giggled.

The teacher met them at the door of the school-house, which was the biggest building at Battle Creek, though it had only one room. She was a plump, middle-aged lady with a watch pinned on the front of her starched white shirtwaist. She shook hands with each pupil and told each where to sit. There were a dozen children in all. Jeff and Maggie turned out to be the entire fourth grade. Joe was in the seventh grade. He sat with three classmates on one of the front benches. After they had sung some songs, the teacher passed out their books. By then it was time for lunch.

They sat on the steps to eat. "I like school," said Maggie. "Last year I didn't miss a single day, except when we were snowed in. As long as the roads are clear I ride to school on my horse Vizzy."

"That's a funny name for a horse," said Jeff.

"It's a funny name for anything," said Joe.

Maggie explained. "His full name is Long Division. I named him that because he's so long that I can divide

91

him up with the Carter girls. We call him Vizzy for short."

Joe had not intended to take part in the conversation, but he could not pass up a chance to talk about horses. "I'm going to name my horse Schoolboy," Joe said, "because he goes to school just like we do."

Jeff objected. "He's not *your* horse any more than he is mine. *I* ought to have a say in naming him."

"He *is* more *my* horse! You don't even know how to ride one."

Jeff did not often get angry, but he did not like to have Joe say such a thing in front of Maggie. He swelled up like a pigeon. "I can ride as well as you can!" he retorted. "*I* never fell off of a horse and lost a race!"

Of course this made Joe furious. He hit out at Jeff, but Jeff dodged him. Maggie stopped them both. "Here comes Teacher!"

By the time school was out Jeff had forgotten all about the quarrel, but Joe was nursing his anger. As soon as they left Maggie and the Carter girls at the crossroads, Joe said, "So you think you can ride a horse as well as I can, do you?"

"Sure I can!" said Jeff stoutly.

"All right, see if you can!" Joe pulled Schoolboy up suddenly. Jeff, taken by surprise, slid backwards to the ground. Joe sat laughing at him.

92

Jeff got up and dusted himself off. He was so angry he could not think. He picked up some stones at the edge of the road and threw them at Joe as hard as he could.

Anger spoiled his aim, and most of the stones struck Schoolboy. With a flirt of his tail and a flip of his heels, the tall, bony horse broke into a run.

In no time at all he was out of sight. Jeff was left alone. Too late he remembered what Big Shorty had told them about running the horse. What if he ran

away with Joe and threw him off? What if Joe was hurt? How would Mamma feel? What would Uncle Boss do? Jeff jogged down the road after Schoolboy, his imagination working faster than his feet.

Faster and faster he ran, and still there was no sign of Joe or Schoolboy. Finally he was so out of breath that he had to sit on a stump and rest. He jumped up as he heard the beat of a horses' hoofs approaching. Yes, it was Joe! Now he would catch it! Jeff thought, but he was so glad to see Joe still alive that he did not care what he did to him.

But Joe did not look at all angry. Instead, he seemed excited and pleased. And he surprised Jeff by begging, "Look, you won't tell Big Shorty I ran the horse, will you? If he knows it he'll take him away from us and we won't get to ride him any more. He sure can run! I'll bet he could beat Chief John's Home Run any day."

Jeff was quick to make use of this opportunity. It was not often that he had the upper hand of Joe.

"Why shouldn't I tell?" he asked. "*I* don't get to ride him, anyway."

"I'll let you ride," said Joe. "You won't tell, will you?"

"You'll have to let me ride in front *half* the time," said Jeff.

Joe scowled, "Oh, all right. I'll ride in front on the

94

way to school, and you can ride him back. If you promise you won't tell."

"I won't tell," grinned Jeff. "Move back. I'm going to ride him right now!"

Jeff climbed on the stump and took his place in the saddle, with Joe behind. To tell the truth, Jeff was not very sure that he *did* know how to ride a horse, but he wasn't going to admit it to Joe. He was careful not to let Schoolboy move faster than a walk.

Jasper, Husky, and Toby met them before they were in sight of camp. Escorted by the dogs, they left Schoolboy at the corral and hurried to the cookhouse. They were as hungry as bears.

The cookhouse was full of warmth and delicious odors. Mrs. Kinnery met them at the door. "How are you, boys? Hurry up and wash your hands. You're just in time to set the table. You'll have to set an extra place tonight. We have company for supper."

9

OLD ANDY

WHEN JEFF went out to call the men to supper, he watched curiously to see who the company would be. He pounded on the triangle, and presently he saw Boss Kinnery coming up the road from the corral with a stranger beside him. The stranger was an old man, very thin, and not nearly as tall as Uncle Boss; but he stepped along as spryly as any of the lumberjacks. Jeff thought this was because of his legs, which were much too long for the rest of him. His head was hunched down into his shoulders, so that he stooped forward. His hair was long and white, and his face was covered with white whiskers. From the waist up he looked very, very old, but from the waist down his long legs marched forward as if he wore seven-league boots.

96

As the old man came up the steps, he stopped and looked at Jeff. "What's this?" he asked Boss. "Hiring 'em young now, ain't you?"

Uncle Boss motioned Jeff out of the way. He started into the house, but the old man stayed, looking Jeff up and down. "Likely looking young 'un," he said. "Is he yourn?"

Uncle Boss turned red. "He's my brother's boy, Andy. There's two of 'em here with their mother. She's cooking for the camp."

The old man chuckled. "Kids and women! Logging ain't what it used to be. Mine's the only business left where a man can get away from 'em!"

"Guess you're right about that."

Jeff followed them inside. While he and Joe served the table they learned more about their guest. The men called him Andy; when they spoke of him they called him Old Andy. He was a prospector.

"What's a prospector?" Jeff asked.

"Mind your manners, Jeff," his mother said. "A prospector is a man who looks for gold."

"If you have any gold in your teeth you'd better keep your mouth shut!" Fred called out. "A friend of mine met up with a prospector once, and he found himself flat on his back with the prospector setting on his chest going after his fillings with a pickax."

Old Andy grinned. Jeff could hardly see his smile

97

for his whiskers, but he could see the twinkle in his blue eyes. "Don't mind him, boy," he told Jeff. "I ain't dangerous. I left my pick out in the corral. Besides, I'm through prospecting now until the snow's come and gone."

"Ve look for snow any day now. Ven Ol' Andy comes down from de mountain every year it better sign for vinter dan vild geese," Ole said.

"That's right," said Mac. "How do you do it, Andy? How do you know when winter will set in?"

"I feel it in my bones," Old Andy answered. "But you needn't start looking for snow just yet. I came down earlier than usual this year. Got some business to attend to."

When supper was over the men usually went at once to their bunkhouses, ready for sleep after a long day's work. But tonight they sat around the table, talking to Old Andy. Mac brought out his bagpipes and gave a concert, marching from one end of the room to the other, and beaming with pleasure to have a chance to show off his skill. Ole whittled in time to the music.

After the concert the men began to swap stories. One would tell a story and then another would think of a better one. Old Andy was full of stories. He kept the men laughing. Jeff and Joe listened from behind the stove. They had finished washing and drying the dishes and setting the table. They crawled back of the stove

98

where the dogs lay drowsing, and sat on the wood box. Their mother sat in a rocking chair darning socks and listening to the men. She had forgotten about bedtime for Jeff and Joe, and they wanted to keep out of sight so that she would not be reminded.

One by one the men yawned and stretched, said good night, and went off to bed. Only Old Andy and Boss Kinnery sat at the table talking, while Mrs. Kinnery nodded in her chair.

Old Andy seemed to have something on his mind. Right in the middle of a story he stopped and asked, "How long is it now that we've known each other, Boss?"

Boss Kinnery pondered. "Why, I don't know, Andy. It must be something like twenty years. When I was working for Old Man Davis over on Clear Creek, you used to come through twice a year and stop at camp for a while, just like you do now."

"That's a fact. Twenty-one years, the way I count it. And how long have you been grubstaking me, Boss?"

Boss Kinnery shifted in his chair. "Aw now, Andy, you couldn't call it grubstaking, exactly. All I've done is let you have some spare groceries now and then."

"Spare groceries! Not to mention the tools and the blankets and the pack animals I've wore out in twenty-one years. Twenty-one years you've been grubstaking me, Boss Kinnery, and you know it!"

"Well, it hasn't hurt me any. And if you ever strike it rich you'll pay me back."

Old Andy nodded. "Sure I will. But I've been doing some thinking lately. All season while I've been up on Snow Mountain, I've been thinking. I ain't as young as I used to be. Suppose I was to die real sudden before I strike it rich? How could I pay you back then for all you've done?

"Aw forget it, Andy!"

"No, sir, I won't forget it. If it hadn't been for you I couldn't 'a kept going all these years. Who else would have trusted me like you have? Why, even my nephew, my own flesh and blood, he turned me down when I needed help most. If you hadn't grubstaked me, I might even 'a had to go to work and live respectable."

Boss Kinnery laughed. Old Andy went on. "I've thought it all out and I've decided what to do. I'm going to pay you back for twenty-one years of vittles and gear. Then I can go back to my diggin's on Snow Mountain next year with a clear conscience."

"I wouldn't take money from you, you old mountain goat—even if you had any!" said Boss Kinnery.

Old Andy chuckled. His bright blue eyes twinkled as if he knew a joke. "Oh, I ain't got no *money!* But I got something else, and I'm going to sign it over to you right now." The old man took a paper from his jacket pocket and unfolded it, spreading it out on the table. "You didn't know I had a tract of timber, did you?"

"No!" said Boss, surprised.

"Well, I do. I homesteaded it before your time. It's mine, all right, and here's the papers to prove it. It's right across the river yonder from where you're cutting now."

"Why, I know that tract! Had my eyes on it for some time. Prettiest stand of timber anywhere around here."

Old Andy smoothed out the paper and wrote something across the bottom of the page with a stubby pencil. With a flourish he signed it. "Glad you like it, 'cause it's yourn, now," he said, handing the paper to Boss Kinnery.

Boss stared at it, his mouth open. He swallowed hard. "I tell you what I'll do," he said. "I'll take your land, and I'll cut the timber. When I sell it, I'll pay you a fair purchase price. That way we'll both come out ahead. How about it?"

"All right with me," Old Andy nodded. "You got the timber and I got a clear conscience. If you make some money for me, too, I'm bound to come out ahead."

The two men shook hands across the table. "I don't mind telling you that this pulls me out of a tight spot," Boss Kinnery said. "I've got more debts than a dog has fleas. It looked like I might have to close down when I
102

finished this job. I was feeling mighty low. But now things look different!"

Jeff and Joe, peeping out from behind the stove, saw Uncle Boss dance a jig in the middle of the floor. He was so big, and his caulked boots made such a noise, that the whole cookhouse shook as if from an earthquake. Jasper woke up and began to howl. Mrs. Kinnery laughed and put away her sewing. Boss and Old Andy laughed, and Jeff and Joe laughed, too.

Then their mother discovered them. "Oh, my gracious!" she exclaimed. "You boys should have been in bed hours ago."

"We wanted to hear Andy talk," Jeff explained.

"Go on to bed, boys," said Old Andy. "I'll be here tomorrow, you know. We'll have a high old time."

10

BUNNY

OLD ANDY was still there when the boys woke up next morning, just as he had promised. In fact, he was sitting by the stove when Jeff and Joe stumbled into the kitchen, rubbing their eyes. He was peeling potatoes.

"Oh!" said Jeff. "We forgot to peel the potatoes last night!"

"Well, you can forget 'em again. I've nearly finished 'em already." He was just taking the last one from the bucket.

"You boys ought to be ashamed, letting Andy do your work for you!" Mrs. Kinnery said, buzzing from the sink to the stove, and from the stove to the table.

Old Andy shook his head. "Oh, I don't need much

sleep these days. Peeling potatoes gave me something to do while I was waiting for daylight. I'll help you with the chores today, Mrs. Kinnery, while the boys are at school."

"Then I'll have time to try out the new harness for my dog team before breakfast!" Joe cried. He was out of the house before his mother could stop him. Pretty soon he was walking up and down the road outside, leading Jasper and Husky hitched to the wagon. Toby was too small for the job, but he ran ahead, barking.

"That boy!" Mrs. Kinnery sighed. "I'm afraid he's going to end up in a circus!"

Old Andy turned to Jeff. "What are *you* going to be when you grow up?" he asked.

"I'm going to be a lumberjack, like Uncle Boss," said Jeff.

His mother smiled sadly. "He's crazy about his Uncle Boss. But Boss doesn't have much use for kids."

"Oh, Boss just talks rough," Old Andy said.

"He says this is no place for the boys."

Old Andy patted Jeff on the shoulder. "He'll change his mind, you wait and see. He'll find out that kids are what makes the world go 'round."

Just as Old Andy spoke this comforting thought, the dogs saw a pack rat dart out from under a bunkhouse and across the road. Excited, they broke away from Joe and dashed after the rat. Boss Kinnery was right in

105

their path; he jumped to avoid the dogs, but lost his balance and fell plop! into the wagon.

His weight slowed the dogs to a stop, but not before Boss had taken an undignified ride past the men who were on their way to breakfast. When he climbed out of the wagon, however, he was not thinking about the ride. He was pointing to the harness. *"Where did you get that leather?"* he demanded, as Joe ran to untangle the dogs.

"Oh, I found it hanging in the barn," Joe answered.

"You've ruined a perfectly good spare harness!"

"I thought nobody was using it."

Uncle Boss waved his arms. "That's just the point! It was supposed to hang there until somebody *did* use it! If you were mine, I'd wear out what's left of that harness on your back!"

Joe faced his uncle, glowering. There was nothing he could say, for he was obviously in the wrong. There was no use trying to convince Boss Kinnery that a dog harness was as important as a team harness. The more Joe realized that he was wrong, the madder he got.

They looked as much alike as a pair of fighting cocks, and there was no telling what might have happened if they had not been interrupted by a loud, rasping noise.

"What's that? What's that?" Jeff cried. He had run out on the steps to see the excitement, and now he started to run toward the corral, where the noise seemed to come from. His mother called him back. "Everybody come and get your breakfast!" she told them. "The food is getting cold."

"But what made the noise?" Jeff asked Old Andy.

"That was Bunny, down at the corral. But don't you let him hear you call it noise. He thinks he's singing."

Joe was sulking on the other side of Old Andy. His lower lip was sticking out, and his hair was standing on end. But Jeff wanted to hear more about Bunny. "Is Bunny a rabbit?" he went on. "Rabbits don't make noises like that—I mean, rabbits don't sing like that."

Old Andy filled his mouth with liver pads and skid-grease. "Well, he has long ears. And he wrinkles his nose. And he likes carrots. So I call him Bunny."

"Can I play with him?"

"We'll go see him right after breakfast," Old Andy promised.

But after breakfast Mrs. Kinnery gave the boys their lunches and told them to hurry or they'd be late to school. Jeff and Joe looked so disappointed that Old Andy said, "Come on. I want to pay a visit to the Agency, anyway. I'll go as far as the crossroads with you."

They went to the corral, where Big Shorty had Schoolboy waiting for them. Beside the tall horse stood a little gray burro. When he saw Old Andy he lifted his head and let out the strange noise that Jeff had wondered about. It sounded like a squeaking wheel or a pump-handle that had not been greased for a long time.

"That's right, Bunny; sing me a song." Old Andy rubbed the burro's long ears. When Jeff and Joe climbed up on Schoolboy, Old Andy mounted Bunny. He did not have to climb; he simply lifted one long leg over Bunny's back, and there he was. As they rode away his feet almost touched the ground.

Schoolboy walked as slowly as he could, and Bunny trotted along by his side. He kept his head close to the ground, watching the road. "Lift your head and look around at the scenery!" Old Andy told him. "You're so used to finding mountain trails where there ain't any that you don't know how to act on a regular road, do you?"

They all stopped to watch a family of squirrels gathering pine nuts. "They'll be hiding out for the winter pretty soon, same as me. But they'll be frisking around again next spring when Bunny and I come back this way." Old Andy tickled Bunny's ear to start him off again.

"Do you go up the mountain every spring, Andy?" Jeff asked.

"Yep. In the old days I wandered all over the country, staying one place one year, another the next. But two - three years ago I made up my mind that what I
108

was looking for was right there on Snow Mountain. I
built me a cabin and now I live like a king every summer while I look around."

"What are you looking for?" Joe was just coming
out of the sulks.

"Gold, of course. I'd pick up silver if I stumbled
over it, but gold is what I'm hunting for, and gold is
what I'll find."

Jeff wondered out loud. "How do you know you'll find it?"

"Well, it's there, isn't it? And if it's there, I'll find it."

"But how do you know it's there?"

"It's got to be there. What's a mountain made of? Why, minerals, of course. What are minerals? Why, gold, and silver, and lead, and iron, and tin, and such like. Well, here's a nice fat mountain. A long time ago it blew up. Yes sir, it blew up, just like those other volcanoes you read about in your geography book. All right, what happened then? Why, all that gold and silver and lead and iron and tin got melted and it boiled over, just like your ma's kettle. It's lying around in the rocks just waiting for me to find it."

"Goodness!" cried Jeff.

Old Andy looked very sly. He chuckled. "I haven't been hunting for gold all my life without learning something. I've figured out just where the richest vein has got to be, and it's not far from my cabin door, either!"

"Where is your cabin?" Joe asked.

"That's one question I don't answer," Old Andy said, looking slyer than ever.

The boys could not get another word out of him on the subject.

Old Andy spent the week at Kinnery Camp. Jeff and

110

Joe enjoyed his visit. They were glad he was there because he helped a lot in the kitchen, doing many of their own chores. But they were also glad just to have him around. Saturday was a wonderful day because there was no school to keep them from spending all their time with Old Andy and Bunny.

Uncle Boss seemed to like having Old Andy around, too. He was in a good humor all week, and whistled cheerfully when he came back from work at night. "We'll start cutting Old Andy's timber right away," he told Mrs. Kinnery. "If we don't have too hard a winter we can have the logs in the river by spring, ready to go down to the mill when the ice thaws. I'll make enough money to pay all my debts and have some left over for—"

"For what, Boss?"

"I've got a use for it, never mind what!"

Mac was the only one who was glad when Old Andy was ready to leave. Not because he didn't like Andy, but because of Bunny. Unfortunately, Bunny had very sharp ears. When Mac marched down the road at night to practice his bagpipes, Bunny could hear him, no matter how far away he went. And when Bunny heard the bagpipes playing, he would lift his head and join in with the most awful braying. He woke up the whole camp.

"He thinks he's singing to the music," Old Andy

111

explained. "He loves to sing better than anything."

"I suppose I'll just have to stop practicing until Bunny is gone," Mac sighed.

When the time came for them to go, Old Andy loaded his belongings on Bunny's back. He looked at the burro's stomach to see how far down it came. He could tell just how heavy the load should be by the curve of Bunny's stomach. He pulled the cinch, but it would not fasten in the old place. Bunny had been leading such an easy life at Kinnery Camp that Old Andy had to let his cinch out a notch.

Jeff and Joe walked part of the way with them as Bunny and Old Andy started off. They waved to them as long as they could see them. "So long!" Old Andy called back. "So long! See you next spring!"

II

THE FIRST SNOW

THE VINE MAPLES under the pines turned as red as flame, so that the whole forest looked as if it were burning up. The dogwood and the alder and the aspen put on their autumn colors. The sun traveled from east to west every day without showing itself above the tops of the trees. Ice began to form at the edge of the creek. Most of the little animals found winter homes for themselves. And Jeff and Joe began to look forward to Christmas.

"Christmas! Why, that's a long way off," said their mother. "You just think about school and learning your lessons."

But the boys had many other things to think about beside school. Getting up at five o'clock on the cold

113

winter mornings, for instance, and carrying water, waiting on table and peeling potatoes! And there were pleasant things to think about, too. Joe had his dog team so well trained now that he could drive the wagon over to Chief John's farm every evening and bring back the milk. Jeff usually went along, and often stayed behind to play with Maggie. Joe would not stay, for every time Chief John saw him he would laugh deep down in his stomach and say something about falling off of a horse. Joe didn't like to be reminded of his fall from Home Run. Every time he thought about it he felt worse.

When Joe was not playing with the dogs he was with Schoolboy. On Saturdays, whenever he could think up an excuse, he rode to the Agency and back. No one bothered any more about whether he ran the horse or not. He managed Schoolboy so well that even Mrs. Kinnery did not worry about him. As for Uncle Boss, he said, "As long as he's on a horse, he's out of trouble." When it was too dark to ride, he curried the horse, and fed him, and watered him, and fussed over him like a mother hen with one chick.

Jeff thought it was more fun to visit the bunkhouses. He visited them all in turn, but he liked best to sit by the stove and talk to Mac and Fred and Chub and Big Shorty and Little Shorty and Ole, all of whom now seemed like old friends. Ole did not talk much, but he whittled the most interesting things with his big knife. He had built shelves above his bunk, and on the shelves he laid out the treasures he had made from bits of wood: picture frames and carved walking canes and boxes and paper-knives.

"What will you do with them, Ole?" Jeff asked.

"Oh, Ay send dem to my people back in Old Country for Christmas," Ole said. He was busy shaping a new piece of wood. As Jeff watched, a small figure of a donkey took form under his knife.

"Why, it looks like Bunny!" Jeff cried. "What are you going to do with *that?*"

"Yoost vait and see!" said Ole.

Jeff sighed. "People always say that!" he complained. "I don't think it's fair!"

But Ole just went on whittling.

It was too cold at night now for Mac to practice his bagpipes outdoors, and there was certainly no room in the bunkhouse for him to practice indoors. So poor Mac laid his pipes away in their box for the winter. He had a deep bass voice, and he liked to sing. Sometimes the others joined in, all but Chub, who could not carry a tune.

Chub liked to talk. The other men had heard all his stories, but Jeff was always ready to listen. "You wouldn't believe it to look at me now," he told Jeff one night, "but I used to be a high-climber in the

115

Douglas fir country across the mountains. I used to climb a hundred and fifty feet up a tree, saw off the top, and dance a jig on the stump."

Jeff gazed at Chub. He was so big around the middle that all his pants had extra pieces sewed in at the waist. He had at least three chins. Jeff could not imagine him climbing a tree, much less dancing a jig high in the air.

"You don't believe me, do you?" Chub accused him. "Of course I was twenty years younger then, and a hundred pounds lighter. With my climbing harness and spikes I could go up a spar tree like a monkey. Have you ever been in the big firs?"

Jeff shook his head.

"Well, they're just about the biggest, oldest, prettiest trees you'll ever see. But they make the toughest logging in the world. And it rains so much on the other side of the mountains that I began to grow moss on my back."

"Is that why you came over here?"

"No, I'd be climbing fir trees yet, I guess, if I hadn't guessed wrong. You see, when you cut the top off the tree, about sixty feet of trunk and branches has got to fall somewhere. It was my business to know which way it would fall. Then I'd get on the other side of the trunk below the cut and hold on while the tree swung back and forth like a steel spring. But one day I didn't figure the fall just right. The cut-off trunk sideslipped

116

and knocked me silly. My life-rope saved me, but I was shook up so bad that I had to lay off for six months. After that I decided I'd rather drive a team."

"What are you going to do when you get too fat to ride a horse?" Little Shorty asked unkindly.

Jeff was called away to do his bedtime chores. He lay awake awhile, listening to the pack rats gnawing somewhere under the house. The cold weather had brought them in. Toby the terrier got so excited when he heard them gnawing that he had been banished to the barn at night. Jasper and Husky did not mind the rats, but slept peacefully as usual at the foot of the boys' bed. Not so Uncle Boss. Jeff could hear him muttering in his room at the other end of the house. Then came the sound of a boot being thrown at the wall. For a few minutes the pack rats were still; then they began again: gnaw, gnaw, gnaw.

Bang! Another of Uncle Boss's heavy caulked boots hit the wall. Husky and Jasper woke and barked as loudly as they could. Nobody could sleep through that racket.

At last silence fell. Even the pack rats were still. It seemed no time at all until the alarm clock went off next morning.

At school the lamps were kept burning all day. In the middle of the afternoon the sky, already a dull gray, grew so dark that the teacher and the pupils all turned at once to look out of the windows. "It's snowing!" cried Jeff.

At first there were only a few crystals on the windowpanes. They melted as they felt the heat from inside. But more flakes came to take their places. Then more and more, until they piled up in little drifts against the glass.

"All the pupils who live outside of Battle Creek may start home now," the teacher announced.

Schoolboy sniffed and snorted and set out for camp at a lope, but Joe pulled him up to keep pace with Maggie's old Vizzy. Joe would have nothing to do with the girls; he thought they were too young and silly to be worth the trouble. Still, he felt that he ought to see that they got safely home through the snow.

At the crossroads, however, they found Chief John coming to meet them on Home Run. "This means the end of the races for this year," he said, looking at the white flakes sifting through the pine needles. "If it lets up tonight, we'll have the last one tomorrow."

Joe did not answer. He looked straight ahead of him with a sulky face.

Chief John said, "Go ahead, girls. Run along with them, Jeff. I'll catch up with you, and you can ride home with us."

Jeff scrambled down and ran beside Vizzy, scooping up handfuls of snow.

Chief John was left alone with Joe. He smiled. He had a kind smile, but Joe wouldn't look at him. Chief John spoke seriously. "Joe, you're a good boy. You've got plenty of nerve. You've got a way with animals. But you've got a mean streak, too. You don't know how to take a joke or a licking. When things get bad, you act worse."

Joe flared up. "Look here! You've got no business—"

"Now, just wait a minute. Get that chip off your shoulder. You think you got a bad break in that race on Home Run, don't you?"

"I did!" cried Joe. "If something hadn't scared him—"

"You think you could win a race, don't you? Would you like another try at it?"

Joe met Chief John's eyes for the first time. "Sure I would."

119

"Well, if we race tomorrow, you can ride Home Run and see what you can do."

"I'll ride Schoolboy!" said Joe. "He can outrun your horse."

"All right. I'll race you myself. But there are two conditions. If you win, you can crow all you want. But if you lose, you got to smile if it kills you. Not one mean look; not one excuse, not one single sulk out of you. If you can't promise that, you can't race."

Joe thought it over. He couldn't imagine smiling if he lost the race. He thought it *might* kill him if he had to smile. He didn't like to lose. But he did want to be in the race. He thought he could win. Finally he muttered, "All right."

Chief John went on. "Another thing. You got to ask your mother before you race. You are figuring on just slipping off and not telling anyone."

Joe turned red. That was exactly what he was figuring on doing.

"You ask her first. It won't hurt you, and it will make her feel better. She'll give you permission."

Joe wasn't so sure. But he had gone too far to back out. "All right," he said again.

Chief John nodded, waved his hand, and cantered off. Home Run was feeling frisky in the snowy weather.

When he got home, Joe went to the cookhouse to carry out his promise to Chief John. He found his
120

mother at the stove, and opened his mouth. It was hard to get the words out. What if she refused to let him race? She helped him out by asking, "What is it, Joe?"

"Chief John says tomorrow will be the last race of the season, and he says I can ride Schoolboy, if you say I can," Joe blurted.

He could tell from her face that she was going to say no. "But Joe—" she began. Then she stopped and began again. "Can't you wait until you're a little older?" She looked at him a long time, and he looked back. She seemed to read in his eyes all the things that he could not say. At last she sighed. "All right. If Chief John says it's all right, I guess it is."

Whew! Joe grinned. That was over. Now for the race!

The next day dawned clear and cold, an ideal day for the last race of the season. After the midday tasks were done, Joe saddled up Schoolboy and rode off to the Agency. Jeff wanted to go along, but Joe wouldn't let him.

There was quite a crowd gathered for the race. As Joe rode up the Indians called out, "That's a mighty long-legged horse! You'll have a long ways to fall before you hit the ground!" Joe felt his red hair begin to stand on end. He started to answer angrily, but he caught Chief John's eye, and clamped his lips together.

Fortunately it was almost time for the race, so he did

121

not have long to hold his temper. There were only three horses racing this time. One run down the track would tell the story.

They lined up at the starting line: Chief John on Home Run, Joe on Schoolboy, and a young Indian on a white-eyed pinto. There were no turns in the road, so it did not matter what position they took. The dirt was firm. The air was crisp and clear. Chief John said to Joe, "How do you feel?"

"I feel fine."

"Does the weather suit you?"

"Sure."

"How about the track?"

"It's in good shape." Joe wondered why he was ask-

ing him so many questions. Was he making fun of him?

Chief John smiled. "I just want to see if you have any excuses, in case you don't win."

Joe was furious. "Don't worry. I'll win!"

"But if you *don't* win, you're going to smile. That's the bargain."

"I said I would, didn't I?" Joe gritted his teeth.

Chief John nodded to the man with the gun, and the starting signal went off. The three horses sprang forward as if they were shot out of the gun themselves.

Joe lay forward, gripping Schoolboy with his knees and giving him loose reins. Schoolboy stretched his long legs and ran. Out of the corner of his eye, Joe could see Home Run's head stretched out almost even

with Schoolboy's. The white-eyed pinto had got off to a faster start than either of them, but almost at once the size of the other two horses began to tell, and the pinto fell back. As they came within sight of the finish line, the race was between Schoolboy and Home Run. First Schoolboy's nose would pull ahead, then Home Run's. Chief John's weight was a handicap, but he and Home Run had run so many races together, and knew each other so well, that they made the most of their chances.

Joe began to hammer Schoolboy with his heels, while Chief John slapped his reins back and forth over Home Run's neck. Still the horses see-sawed for the lead.

The faces on each side of the road went by in a blur of color and noise. There was the finish line. Home Run gave a great leap, and he was over first.

Joe drew Schoolboy in as soon as he could, but he wished that he could just gallop on and on, and never go back. He hated to face the crowd. He hated to face Chief John. He dismounted and led the horse slowly back. To his surprise, people came crowding around him, patting him on the back and telling him what a good race he had run. Joe could not look at them. Then he saw Chief John waiting for him, holding out his hand. This was the bad moment. He had to keep his bargain.

124

Joe tried to smile. His face felt stiff. It really hurt to move his lips. He broke into a cold sweat. Still Chief John stood looking at him, holding his hand so that he could not get away.

"It was a good race, Joe," Chief John said.

Joe made a great effort. His face stretched into something that would pass for a smile. Chief John shook his hand warmly. Everyone gathered around the two of them, talking about the horses and their riders. "The fastest time we've ever had," someone said. "That's a smart horse of yours, Chief John," someone else said, "but if the track had been fifty yards longer, this long-legged horse and this red-headed kid would have beat you."

Joe spoke without thinking. "Oh, I don't know about that!"

Chief John looked at him. Joe blushed all over. He grinned, and suddenly it wasn't any trouble to smile.

12

THE CHRISTMAS TREE

W HEN the news of the race reached Kinnery Camp, the lumberjacks teased Joe, as usual. "First thing you know we'll be famous for being the home of Joe Kinnery, the great jockey," Chub said. Fred added, "We'll have to build a room onto the cookhouse to hold all his prizes!"

But Joe did not go off and sulk as usual. He looked the men in the eye. "Chief John says I'm going to grow too big to be a jockey," he said. "But Schoolboy will win next year, you see if he doesn't!"

Boss Kinnery turned to look at Joe. "What's got into you?" he asked. "What's happened to that lower lip we've been tripping over all summer?"

Joe felt his hair bristle, but he bit his tongue to keep

126

from making an angry answer. Instead, when the men laughed, he tried to laugh too.

His uncle stopped laughing, and that was the last of the jokes about horse races. The men were working very hard to cut as many logs as possible before the winter closed in. So far, the snow was not too deep. The teams went out every morning with the snowplow to clear the roads. But it was cold work. During the day when the sun was warm, their clothes were soaked with melted snow. Early in the afternoon, everything froze solid again. The men came back to camp stiff and sore. After supper they went at once to their bunks to keep warm. The wind whistled through the bunkhouses, and the cookhouse was not much warmer.

At school the children began to talk about Christmas. First it was a month away, then three weeks, then two. A week before Christmas the holidays began.

Jeff, Joe, and Schoolboy slogged home through the snow. It was packed deep on the ground, and above the packed snow was a layer of fresh snow, growing deeper by the minute. The snow kept falling.

They put Schoolboy in the barn and patted Jasper, Husky, and Toby, who had come out to meet them. Aside from the dogs there seemed to be no one around. It was already dark, but only one of the bunkhouses showed light and smoke. The boys waded through the snow to the cookhouse.

127

As always, the kitchen was filled with good warm cooking smells. As always, Mrs. Kinnery had a smile for Jeff and Joe. But the long table was set for only five places. Boss Kinnery was sitting in the rocking chair beside the stove in his stocking feet, greasing his boots.

"Where is everybody?" Jeff asked.

Uncle Boss told him, "We've shut down. No use to work good men in this weather. Everybody's gone into town but Ole."

"They'll be back in the spring," Mrs. Kinnery said. "Ole didn't care about going, so he's staying here to help out around the place."

"Ole and I can look out for ourselves, I tell you, Polly," Boss said. "You'd better take the boys and go into town, too, before we get snowed in."

"We'd just as soon stay here, wouldn't we, boys?"

"Sure we would."

Uncle Boss frowned. "Well, I might as well tell you that we're likely to have a thin time of it. Paying off the men leaves me flat broke. Until I get Old Andy's timber to the mill I won't have a dime."

"We've got one ham left. We'll have it for Christmas. There's bacon and potatoes and canned goods and the stuff from Chief John's farm. We'll make out. Maybe it will be an early spring." Mrs. Kinnery smiled.

Jeff said, "Let's get a Christmas tree tomorrow!"

Next morning when Jeff and Joe went outside, they

128

stepped directly into a snowbank. The snow was level with the door sill. The dogs floundered in it; Toby almost disappeared. Joe rescued him and he went yelping back into the house. Old Jasper sneezed at it and licked his paws. He did not like it at all, and retired with dignity to his favorite place behind the stove. But Husky, with his thick shaggy coat, went plowing and frisking through the snow as if he thought it had been put there just for him.

Armed with an ax and a saw, the boys set out to find a Christmas tree. There were plenty of little pines around the camp, but they wanted a fir tree. They remembered some firs across the creek, so they walked that way. Halfway up the hill on the other side they found one they liked. It was just the right size and just the right shape. Jeff trimmed off the lowest limbs, and Joe said, "Stand back, now, I'll show you how to cut it down."

"I know how to cut it down! I've watched the men. I can do it as well as you can."

"Aw, you're too little."

This was the kind of treatment that set off Jeff's temper like a skyrocket. He grabbed at the saw. Joe was too strong for him, of course, and he pushed Jeff into the snow while he went on sawing. Jeff picked up the ax and fell to work on the other side of the tree, chopping as fast as he could in hope that he would beat

129

Joe. In the excitement of the race they both forgot their anger and it became a game. The saw whined; the chips flew. Crack! Suddenly the trunk staggered, snapped, and collapsed on top of them both. The thick branches slapped them off their feet; they fell, their faces pressed into the snow.

Horrible thoughts of broken bones and suffocation filled both their minds as they struggled to get out from under the tree. Joe, coming to the surface, cried, "Jeff! Jeff! Where are you?"

"Where do you think I am?" Jeff's head popped up.

On their feet again, they looked at the fallen tree. It was much longer and heavier than they had expected. They tugged at it, but it was hard to budge.

"How are we going to get it home?" Jeff wondered.

While the boys stood looking at the tree, Maggie came floundering down the hill.

"What are *you* doing here?" Joe demanded impolitely.

Maggie stuck out her tongue at Joe. "What are *you* doing?"

130

Jeff told her, "We came to cut a Christmas tree, but now we can't figure out how to get it home."

"It would be easy if you had a sled," Maggie said.

"A sled! Of course!" Jeff cried.

Joe didn't say anything for a while. He hated to admit that Maggie had thought of something before he did. Finally he said, "But we *don't* have a sled."

"Well, you can make one, can't you?"

"Come on!" Jeff and Maggie led the way up to the farm. Chief John was chopping wood at the woodpile. When Maggie explained their plan, her father took them to the barn and brought down some old boxes from the loft.

"Here you are," he told them. "You can get the boards and nails out of these. You've got a saw, and here's a hammer. Let's see what you can do."

Joe knew just what to do. "You can pull the nails out of boxes and hammer 'em straight," he told Maggie. "I guess you know enough to do that." He showed Jeff how long to measure the planks. He sawed the planks himself, because he said they couldn't do that right. Before they knew it the sled was taking shape.

"I'm making it extra long so it will hold the tree," Joe explained.

"I bet it would hold all three of us!" Jeff cried.

"Let's try it!" Maggie suggested.

Joe put a few finishing touches on the sled, smooth-

131

ing off the runners with his knife. Then they dragged it up the slope behind the farm.

"It's hard to climb in the snow," puffed Jeff. "But the higher we climb the farther we can slide."

They got on the sled. There was room enough for all of them if they squeezed up close.

"Pick up your feet!"

"Hold tight!"

"Let's go!"

"Ooooooooooooo!"

The cold wind stung their faces and brought tears to their eyes. The white snow slid past them so fast that the whole world seemed to be left behind. There was no way to guide the sled and no way to stop it. They just had to hold on until they came to level ground.

"My, that's fun!"

"It's better than riding a horse!"

"It's better than flying!"

"Let's do it again!"

They did it again and again. They had so much fun that they lost track of time. Then, as they were picking themselves up from a tumble, they heard Chief John calling from the farm. At the same time they heard the "bing-bing-bing" of the triangle being beaten at the camp. It was lunchtime.

Soaked with snow, out of breath, and very, very

hungry, the boys burst through the cookhouse door.

"Well!" said their mother. "Where's the Christmas tree?"

Jeff and Joe looked at each other. "We forgot all about it!" They told their mother and Uncle Boss and Ole about the sled they had made, and all the fun they had had coasting. "We'll get the tree this afternoon."

Ole went with them to get the tree, and before dark they had it standing in one corner of the cookhouse. It filled the room with the fragrance of the forest. Even Uncle Boss said it looked pretty.

He had been to the Agency for some supplies, driving a team hitched to the sleigh. "If it snows tonight we won't be able to keep the road clear," he said. "The horses could hardly break a trail today."

It did snow that night. It snowed day after day and night after night. But the long hours indoors were busy ones just the same. Ole whittled and Uncle Boss went over his accounts and Mrs. Kinnery knitted. The horses munched and stamped in the barn. The dogs slept hour after hour behind the stove. The creatures of the woods huddled in their dens. The pack rats gnawed under the floors. Jeff and Joe made decorations for the Christmas tree.

They dipped pine cones in whitewash and hung them on the tree. They strung ropes of red cranberries and wound them round and round. They borrowed

133

the tin snips from the blacksmith's shop and cut out dozens of shiny stars from empty tin cans. The tree twinkled in the lamplight.

The last touch was added when Jeff decked the tree with colored paper chains. Mrs. Kinnery stopped her work to admire it. "Where did you get the colored paper for the chains?" she asked.

"I found it," said Jeff. "Isn't the tree pretty?"

"It's a beautiful tree. Now run and get me a can of tomatoes from the shelf."

Jeff went to the storeroom. He didn't come out for some time. "Jeff! What's the matter with that boy?" his mother called. "Why don't you bring the can of tomatoes?"

Jeff's voice answered, sounding very small. "I-I can't find it."

"What do you mean, you can't find it? They're right there on the shelf with the corn and peaches and beans." Mrs. Kinnery went into the storeroom to see what was the matter.

She found Jeff staring at the shelves. The cans were there, all right, row after row of them, but the bright-colored labels had been taken off. They were just bare cans, and no one could tell one from the other.

"I used the colored labels for the paper chains!" wailed Jeff.

13

CHRISTMAS

EARLY Christmas morning the ham went into a big boiler. "We'll have dinner this evening," Mrs. Kinnery announced. "That's a fine ham. After I boil the salt out of it and bake it with apples, we'll have the best Christmas dinner in the country!"

"You're bragging, Polly!" Uncle Boss teased her.

She stuck up her chin. "Well, I *am* a good cook, and I don't mind saying so!" she smiled. "You wait till you taste that ham!"

"Well, don't make us wait until evening, then!"

"Now, Boss, cooking takes time. You'll get it when it's ready."

Ole came in for breakfast, carrying a big cardboard box. He set it carefully down on a bench. The boys kept looking at it while they ate. Nobody had said anything about presents. They knew that times were hard and that they should not expect anything this year. Still, they couldn't help wondering what Ole had in that box.

After he had eaten, Ole rose slowly and stood looking at the boys. Without a word, he carried the bench and the box and placed them beside the tree. Slowly he opened the box and reached inside.

He brought out the little wooden donkey and put it on the bench. Reaching in again, he brought out a carved wooden lamb. One by one he produced a whole series of animals, putting them carefully in a semicircle on the bench. The boys came close to watch him.

The little figures were beautifully carved. Each one had its own small platform so that it would stand up. By the time Ole had brought out some figures of people, Uncle Boss and Mrs. Kinnery had come over to see what he was doing, too.

"It's going to be like a picture in a book, Mamma!" Jeff cried. "It's going to be the story of Bethlehem. See, there are the animals, and the Wise Men!"

"And there are the Angels!"

"And there are Mary and Joseph!"

"All it needs is the Baby!"

Ole, who had not said a word, was enjoying the effect of his surprise. His hollow-cheeked face could not look any way but mournful, but his eyes were as clear and bright as a child's. He paused dramatically. Then he held up the last piece between his thumb and forefinger. It was a tiny cradle, with a tiny Baby inside, no bigger than a button. He placed it beside the figure of Mary.

"Oh, Ole! It's the prettiest thing I ever saw," Mrs. Kinnery said.

"Ve make dese in Old Country," Ole beamed. "Every house have vun at Christmas. My family make dem long time. My grandfather carve one like dis for King."

Jeff and Joe had to look at each piece by itself, and replace them in various positions. Then they helped with the chores at the barn, and then they were hungry. While Mrs. Kinnery made them some sandwiches, Chief John and Maggie came in, powdered with new-fallen snow. They brought some milk and eggs, and Chief John stayed to talk business with Uncle Boss. Ole was whittling again in a corner.

Mrs. Kinnery called to the children. "Go out to the water barrel and wash those hands before you eat. And when you come in, bring another bucket of water for the ham." She poured off the salt-water, and clouds of wonderful-smelling steam rose from the boiler.

"What are you going to have for Christmas dinner?" Jeff asked Maggie as they washed their hands. There was a shelf with a basin and a bar of soap next to the water barrel. They had to break through an inch of ice to fill the basin and the bucket.

"We're not going to have any," Maggie answered. "Mother and the girls and the baby went to visit Brother a week ago. Now they're snowed in and can't get back. My daddy and I will eat beans."

Jeff was horrified. No Christmas dinner? He whispered the story to his mother as Joe helped pour the water over the ham. She said at once, "Why, Chief John, you and Maggie must have dinner with us!"

"Sure!" agreed Uncle Boss. "What's a Christmas dinner without company?"

So it was arranged. While the men went outside to shovel out the paths, the children stayed indoors to help Mrs. Kinnery. There were apples to peel and walnuts to crack. "I'll see if the ham has boiled enough," Mrs. Kinnery said after a while. "When it's ready to bake, you can stick the cloves on top."

She took the lid off the boiler. Instead of a cloud of steam, a mountain of white suds boiled out of it, seething and bubbling all over the stove. Instead of a delicious fragrant odor of ham, the room was filled with a strong smell of soap.

For a moment they could do nothing but stare at the mess. Then Mrs. Kinnery lifted the boiler off the stove and sniffed at it. "Soap! Now, how in the world could soap get into my boiler?"

139

She looked at the children, who were looking at each other. They remembered the bar of soap beside the water barrel. Mrs. Kinnery understood.

She took the ham out of the boiler and poured clean water over it and sniffed it again. "Soap! It still smells

of soap," she wailed. "It's ruined! What will we have for Christmas dinner?" She wrung her hands.

Joe said, "We'll eat it anyway, Mamma!"

She shook her head. "It'll taste of soap. Your Uncle Boss will never let me hear the last of this. After I bragged so much about my cooking!"

"We'll eat beans, Mamma; we like beans, don't we?" Jeff tried to comfort her, and the others joined in. "Oh, yes, beans are good, 'specially with that hot-sauce you make."

Mrs. Kinnery stopped wringing her hands and gave the ham another look. "Hot-sauce! I wonder. . . ." She thought a few moments, while Jeff and Joe and Maggie held their breath. "That's it! I'll boil it again, and then I'll bake it in hot-sauce. Nobody will taste soap when I get through with it!"

She plunged into work, and the children flew to get the things she called for. "Onions! Pepper! Flour! Catsup!" They worked so fast that when the men came back, the ham was already in the oven bubbling in its sauce. Mrs. Kinnery was darning peacefully in her rocking chair, and Jeff and Joe and Maggie were setting the table.

Uncle Boss drew a deep breath. "Mmm! Smells good in here!"

"We'll be ready to eat by the time you men get washed up," Mrs. Kinnery said.

They all sat down to Christmas dinner. The ham was placed before Boss Kinnery at the head of the table. All eyes were upon him as he carved the pink juicy slices and put them on the plates. Over each slice he poured a ladleful of rich brown sauce. Mrs. Kinnery and the children watched anxiously while the men took their first bites. Smiles of appreciation beamed from each face.

"Ahhh!" sighed Uncle Boss. "I always said you were a good cook, Polly!"

Mrs. Kinnery gave a sigh of relief. Jeff, Joe, and Maggie started to giggle. Then nobody said anything for a while. They were all too busy eating.

The boys had a secret which they had kept for a week now, and they could not keep it any longer. As soon as dinner was over they brought out the presents they had made at school and handed them around. Joe had made calendars for everyone, and Jeff had made bookmarks. He had taken great pains with them, making each of a different color, with each person's name printed with crayons. He had admired them very much, but just now, as he presented them, an awful thought struck him. Maybe people wouldn't like them! Maybe they didn't have any books!

He looked so sad that Ole guessed what he was worrying about. "Dat's fine!" he exclaimed, holding up his bookmark. "Ay keep it in my Bible."

"Do you have a Bible?" Jeff asked. "I never saw it."

"Ay keep it under pillow," Ole whispered to Jeff. "Ay read it every night; now Ay can mark de place."

Jeff felt better. Chief John told him, "I'll use mine in my almanac. I've needed a marker for a long time, to mark the page where the horse diseases are."

And Mrs. Kinnery said, "I'll use mine in my cookbook, to mark the hot-sauce recipe!"

Maggie was not to be outdone. She brought out of her father's mackinaw pocket a box of homemade candy she had hidden there. "I made it myself!" she said. "There's some for everybody." She added, "Joe can have some, too."

"I have something for everybody, too," said Mrs. Kinnery. And she produced from her hiding place a wonderful assortment of mittens, socks, and stocking-caps, all knitted warmly of bright red wool. "Just try them on and take the one that fits best," she told them.

This took quite a while, and caused a great deal of laughter. Uncle Boss couldn't find a thing to fit him, so he put Maggie's mittens on his ears for ear muffs. And one sock was so big that nobody could think of any use for it until Jeff tried it on Toby, the terrier. With the foot cut off, it made a fine sweater for him.

"It must be getting late," Chief John said at last. He tried to look out of the window. But there was nothing outside but snow. The drifts had piled up until

143

the house was buried to the eaves in fresh white snow.

They all bundled up to go outside with Chief John and Maggie. Uncle Boss gave them a shovel to take with them, to clear the drifts from the path. They started home, and the others called after them, "Merry Christmas! Merry Christmas!"

Mrs. Kinnery went with Jeff and Joe and the men to see that everything was all right in the barn. The barn was buried in tall drifts, too, but inside the animals were dry and warm. Jeff held the lantern while Joe patted Schoolboy's nose and put Toby on his bed of hay. "Merry Christmas!" they told the animals, "Merry Christmas!"

Outside again the stars were so clear and bright that they lit up the snow. Ole said good night and went to his bunkhouse, where a fire in the wood stove was roaring away trying to keep out the drafts. "Merry Christmas, Ole!" everybody said. "Merry Christmas!" he called after them.

Going back to the cookhouse, Uncle Boss said, "That was a mighty good dinner, Polly."

Mrs. Kinnery answered softly, "Thank you, Boss. And we all had fun, didn't we?"

"You bet we did."

"Aren't you glad you didn't send the boys away?" Uncle Boss hesitated. "Come on, Boss, admit it!" Mrs. Kinnery coaxed.

The boys waited to hear his answer. He cleared his throat. "Oh, well, sure; kids are all right—at Christmas!" he said. Then he spoiled it. "But Christmas comes just once a year."

145

14

SLATS

ALTHOUGH the boys had another week of holidays, their mother began at once to worry about how they were going to get back to school. The snow was much too deep for walking, and even if the snowplow could break out the road, it would be hard going for Schoolboy. There was the sleigh and the team, but Uncle Boss and Ole were using them to get in a supply of firewood.

Mrs. Kinnery worried about it out loud while she cooked. "It won't hurt 'em to miss school for a while," Boss answered. Mrs. Kinnery flared up. "Don't you dare say that, Boss Kinnery!" she cried. "These boys are going to get an education. They're going to have a better education than you or I ever had! Miss school?

I'll carry them there myself before they'll miss school."

Uncle Boss just smiled. "If you had left them in town they wouldn't have any trouble getting to school. I told you—"

Mrs. Kinnery turned her back on him.

Ole put away his whittling and stood up. "Ay got idea," he said. "Yeff, Yoe—yu come wit me."

Wondering, Jeff and Joe put on their jackets and followed Ole to his bunkhouse. There, Ole reached under his bunk and brought out two long, flat wooden objects.

"What in the world are those? They look like bed slats, Ole!"

"Dese slats vill take yu to school, Yoe. Ay make some like dem for yu and Yeff."

"Take us to school, Ole? What do you mean?"

"How can bed slats take us to school?"

For answer, Ole carried the boards outside. Then he knelt down and fastened them to his feet. "Ve call dem skis," he explained. He showed the boys how he could walk on them, lifting one forward, then the other, keeping them parallel in the snow. "In Old Country ve use dem all vinter. Mamma, papa, kids—ever'boty use dem."

Using a pair of slender poles to help him along, Ole walked to the path where the ground sloped down toward the creek. Then suddenly he bent his knees, gave

147

a push with his poles, and went sliding down the hill.

Jeff and Joe gasped. They watched him speed over the snow, going faster and faster the farther he went. "He's headed straight for that tree!" cried Jeff. "Oh! He missed that one, but there's another!"

"Look at him go!" yelled Joe.

Ole sailed like a bird over the snow, zigzagging between the trees. He came up with a swoosh at the bottom of the hill. The boys plunged down to meet him.

"How do you do it?"

"It looked like you were flying!"

"Can you teach us how?"

Ole showed them how to climb up the hill, placing his skis at an angle so that they made a sort of crow's-foot track. "Sure Ay teach yu how. Ve practice a while right now. Den later Ay make skis for both."

First Joe and then Jeff tried out the skis. But they did not fly like birds down the hill. Ole made them practice on the level ground. They learned to walk and to turn around without tangling their skis. Even at that, they spent more time in the snow than on top of it.

When Mrs. Kinnery saw what they were doing she came to the door to stop them. "Jeff! Joe! What in the world are you doing? You'll break your legs!"

"We're skiing, Mamma!"

"Well, don't do it. It looks dangerous to me."

Joe explained, "But Ole says we can go to school this way."

"Ole!" Mrs. Kinnery scolded. "What do you mean by fooling those boys?"

Ole defended himself. "No, ma'am. Ay voodent fool 'em for nutting! Ay go to school myself dis vay ven Ay was liddle boy."

Mrs. Kinnery appealed to Uncle Boss. "Boss, make them stop! It's dangerous."

Uncle Boss grumbled. "First you say you want them to go to school, and then you say they can't. You have to make up your mind."

Mrs. Kinnery thought a moment. "Can they *really* go to school on those things?"

"It's just about the only way they *can* go."

"All right then," she agreed. "Go ahead and learn to ski. Go ahead and teach them, Ole. But I'm afraid to watch." She went back into the house.

Before darkness fell the boys had learned to keep their footing on level ground. "Yu do goot," Ole told them. "Yu do better ven yu get skis of your own. Next veek yu ski to school."

Jeff and Joe practiced most of the time during the next few days, and Ole worked most of the time on their skis. When these were ready, the lessons went much faster. By the end of the week they had made the trip to Chief John's farm on skis. They looked long-

149

ingly at the white hillside behind the barn. "I'll take the sled and you go on your slats," Maggie told them. "Let's see who gets to the bottom of the hill first."

They tried it. The boys discovered that the skis were much more fun than the sled, for they could guide themselves and control their speed by the way they shifted their weight. But Maggie preferred the sled. "I like to have something between me and the snow," she said.

On Saturday Ole, Jeff, and Joe skied to the Agency and back. Joe fell down only twice, and Jeff fell down only three times. But one of the times was while he was carrying eggs.

Next day the boys made the most of their last holiday. They would hardly leave their skis long enough to eat.

"They certainly have learned fast," their mother said admiringly.

"Dey are mighty likely young'uns," Ole agreed. He was pleased with his pupils. "Look at dem now!"

The snow had been shoveled away from the window, and they could look out and see Jeff and Joe at the barn. Joe climbed up to the top of the roof. The sides were covered with the deep drifts, but the roof sloped steeply from the ridge. Joe almost lost his balance as he made ready to slide. He caught himself, though, and went down, swoop! and around, swoosh!

to a perfect stop. He looked very proud of himself.

"If Joe does it, of course Jeff's determined to do it,"
Mrs. Kinnery sighed. Sure enough, there went Jeff up
on the roof. "I can't help thinking that it's very dangerous."

"It takes de knowing how," Ole agreed.

Uncle Boss came to see what they were looking at.
"Oh, I don't see what you're so excited about," he
said. "Anybody can slide down a barn roof."

"It's easy ven yu slide on seat of pants. But on skis
yu got to know how."

"I don't see that there's much to know," Uncle Boss
argued.

"I guess yu t'ink yu can do it?" Ole asked, a gleam
in his eye.

Down went Jeff from the top of the roof. Swoop!
Swoosh! It did look easy.

Mrs. Kinnery said, "You'd better not try it, Boss.
You're not as young as you were."

That was the last straw. "Come on!" said Uncle
Boss. "Just fasten those things on my feet, and I'll
show you."

Ole tried to talk him out of the idea, but Boss led
the way to the barn, climbed to the top and had Ole's
skis fastened to his boots. Jeff and Joe watched, open-
mouthed. Mrs. Kinnery watched from the kitchen
window.

151

Boss stood up, and down he went. At first everything went well. Then his skis got crossed, and he went head over heels into the snow. Ole, Jeff, and Joe ran to pull him out.

"Are you all right?" Jeff asked.

"Of course I'm all right!" he answered crossly. "Think a little tumble like that would hurt me?"

But he limped back to the cookhouse. And for a whole week he had a hard time getting into and out of a chair.

152

15

SIGNS OF SPRING

DURING the winter skiing got to be an old story
to the boys. Every morning after the breakfast chores
were done, they put on their jackets, their boots, their
scarves, mittens, and caps with flaps over the ears. They
buckled on their skis and set out for school.

On skis they did not need to follow the road, so they
usually took the shorter way over Battle Ridge. The
hill was named, like the settlement at Battle Creek, for
a battle between the soldiers and the Indians during
one of the old Indian wars. Much of the timber in this
area had been cut, leaving clear slopes for skiing. The
climb was steep, however, and Jeff and Joe were warm
by the time they reached the top. They always rested
a moment at the top of the ridge. On clear days they
could look back over the way they had come. They

could see the smoke from Kinnery Camp and from Chief John's farm. Beyond, they saw the cold white peak of Snow Mountain, with the sunrise turning the sky pink behind it.

Then they pushed off down the hill. The wind whistled past their ears, and the moisture in their eyes and nostrils froze. Their breath was snatched out of their mouths in little white clouds.

Once down Battle Ridge, the trail went under the big trees where sometimes the overloaded branches would dump their snow upon the boys as they glided past. The forest was so silent that the schoolroom always seemed very noisy and crowded when they reached it. It was good to warm their hands and feet at the glowing stove, though, and to see their friends.

So the winter passed. It seemed like a long time; and yet before they knew it the snow had melted from the trees, and the drifts had withdrawn from the houses. At night Jeff could hear the wild geese flying over the camp. Toby, the terrier, was able to run about outdoors again, and he began to find the tracks of little animals coming out from their winter quarters. The deer, who had come right up to the barnyard searching for food during the coldest weather, went back to their high grazing grounds.

Another sign of spring was the return of the lumberjacks. Most of the old ones came back—Fred and Chub

and Little Shorty and Big Shorty and Mac and his bag-pipes. There were some new men, too, who ate just as much as the old ones. Mrs. Kinnery was cooking again from morning till night. Jeff and Joe were up to their ears again in potatoes. Uncle Boss had to borrow money in town to lay in supplies for the season. Still, he was in a good humor, thinking of Old Andy's timber, which would solve all his problems. He and the men built a log bridge across the river and moved into the virgin forest. Axes rang and saws whined. Whips cracked and the big wheels turned. "There's nothing to stop us now!" Uncle Boss crowed.

Then, to prove that spring had really arrived, Old Andy himself came up the road one noonday, walking as spryly as ever beside Bunny. It was Sunday, so the boys saw him coming, and everybody in camp came out to meet him. Jeff and Joe took charge of Bunny. They led him to the corral, took off his pack, and gave him a trough full of oats. He was as round as a butter-ball from his winter of ease, but he fell to munching greedily, as if he knew that his rations would not be so plentiful from now on.

Uncle Boss offered to take Old Andy over to the logging area to see how the work was getting on. The old man shook his head. "I never did enjoy seeing a tree cut down," he said. "I'll stay here and visit with Mrs. Kinnery and the boys."

This suited Jeff and Joe. They had so much to show Old Andy and so much to tell him. They were disappointed when they found out that he planned to leave next day. "Why do you have to go?" Jeff asked.

"I got some looking to do," Old Andy said.

"But you don't have to go tomorrow," Joe said. "Snow Mountain is not going to move away."

Old Andy looked off at the mountain. "I guess Snow Mountain will be there quite a spell," he agreed. "But I got a feeling that *I* won't be around much longer. I got a feeling that if I'm going to find that gold, I'd better find it this summer."

"But couldn't you wait a little while?" Jeff begged.

The old prospector shook his head. "I get kind of an itch in my feet this time of year," he murmured. "Bunny, he's just the same. He's been prancing in his stall for a month now, trying to tell me it was time to go. Him and me have been together so long, we each know what the other is thinking."

"How long have you owned him, Andy?"

"I don't know whether *I* own him or *he* owns *me*. We've been together fifteen years now. Bunny's getting along in years, too. But he'll outlive me. And he'll never leave me until I'm dead."

The boys didn't like to hear Old Andy talk like that, but he seemed as cheerful as ever. At the supper table he kept everybody laughing with his jokes and stories.

157

The men joked with him, trying to get him to tell where his cabin was up on the mountain. But he would not give his secret away. "Nobody knows but me and Bunny!" was all that he would say.

After the men had gone to their bunks, Boss Kinnery showed Old Andy his ledger, and promised, "I'll have the purchase price of your timber ready for you when you come down next fall. We'll both have some cash for a change."

Old Andy said, "I ain't worried about the money, Boss. That timber belongs to you. I gave it to you and you got a paper that proves it, legal."

"Well, hit the hay, everybody," Boss Kinnery yawned. "Let's get some sleep."

Everyone went to bed, but it was not so easy to go

to sleep. First they heard Mac's bagpipes. He had forgotten about Bunny! Sure enough, like an echo, Bunny's hee-haw! hee-haw! split the air. The dogs barked mightily. Presently the noises died away. Jasper and Husky stopped barking and curled up again. Old Andy began to snore. He snored almost as loudly as Bunny brayed. Then Toby started to bark outside Uncle Boss's room. He had left his bed in the barn and was after the pack rat gnawing under the floor. The rat gnawed and scampered, while Toby whined, barked, and scratched outside the house.

Uncle Boss threw a boot at the floor. The rat quieted down, and after a while Toby did, too. Old Andy turned over, and his snores sank to a peaceful purr. At last silence fell upon Kinnery Camp.

Next day Old Andy went away. The boys walked with him as far as Chief John's farm. Maggie came out to tell Old Andy good-by. The old prospector shaded his eyes and looked up toward the top of Snow Mountain. The lower slopes were green now, but the mountain was still covered with snow far below the timberline. Old Andy took up a sturdy new walking stick which Ole had made for him.

"Come on, Bunny," he said. "Let's go find that gold!"

Jeff, Joe, and Maggie stood looking after the old man and the little burro. They watched until they had disappeared among the trees. They went off to school, still thinking about their old friend. That evening when the boys came back to the farm to get the milk, they stopped again to look up at the mountain. It was too dark to see anything but a great mass of dark green trees and cold blue snow. But somewhere on the side of the mountain they saw a tiny bright spark.

"There's Old Andy's campfire!" Maggie cried.

"I wonder where his cabin is?" said Joe.

"I hope he finds that gold," Jeff murmured.

160

16

MISSING

JASPER, Husky, and Toby would not let any other dogs into camp. Although they had once been strays themselves, they now looked upon all stray dogs as their enemies. If any one of them saw a strange dog approaching the camp, he would bristle and growl, and the other two would come running to help him chase the stranger away.

Sometimes the visiting dog would stand his ground. In that case there would be a battle. Jasper, Husky, and Toby showed the scars of many such battles, but they never lost one. They remained rulers of Kinnery Camp.

One evening, however, they met their match. Jasper often went off into the woods on hunting trips of his own. He had a deep voice, and whenever he found an animal he could be heard following it for miles, baying as he went. On this occasion, about two weeks after Old Andy's departure, Jeff and Joe, peeling potatoes in the cookhouse, heard him coming toward camp, barking excitedly. "Let's see what he's got!" cried Joe. They dashed out of the house, followed by Husky and Toby.

"Here he comes!"

Out of the woods scuttled a fearful-looking little animal, a bundle of long quills standing out like angry needles. "It's a porcupine!" said Joe. "I hope Jasper knows enough not to get too near *him!*"

Jasper came out into the open. He was barking with all his might, but he was an old hound, and he had learned about porcupine quills a long time ago. He kept his distance. Husky had had experience with porcupines, too. He stayed behind the boys and added his

voice to the uproar. The porcupine, hearing dogs on all sides of him, made for the first refuge he saw. He scurried under the barn.

Toby saw him go. Toby was a young dog, and if he had ever been told anything about porcupines, he did not stop to remember it now. Barking furiously, he scrambled under the barn after him.

"Come back here!" Joe yelled. "Come back here this minute!"

But it was too late. There was a growling and a snarling. Then the most piercing yelping. Then out shot poor Toby like a bullet, his tail between his legs. His head was covered with porcupine quills.

Jeff and Joe caught him. Joe held him between his legs and he and Jeff pulled out the quills one by one. It was a painful lesson for young Toby. Each quill brought a yelp from the dog and a wince from Jeff and Joe. Jasper and Husky sat nearby to watch. They looked

very mournful and sympathetic, and whimpered softly.

They were almost through with this unhappy task when the sound of steps attracted their attention. They did not sound like human footsteps, yet they were not quite like a horse's hoofbeats, either. The boys and the dogs stared at the woods behind the barn, where the sound seemed to be. Soon they saw what was making it. "Bunny!" cried both boys at once.

Bunny came to the corral fence, hung his head over the top rail, twitched his long ears, wrinkled his soft gray nose, and let out a loud "Hee-haw!"

Jeff asked, "Where's Old Andy?"

Joe went to the burro. Around his neck hung a broken rope. "He's run away! Maybe Old Andy is hurt. You put Bunny in the corral, Jeff, and then run and tell Mamma. I'll look around and see if Old Andy's anywhere near."

Jeff burst into the cookhouse. "Mamma! Mamma! Bunny has come back and Old Andy isn't with him!"

Mrs. Kinnery threw a coat over her shoulders and came out with Jeff. On the way to the barn they met Uncle Boss and the men coming from work. They explained what had happened, and everybody went to the corral to see Bunny. They stood around him, asking questions as if he could answer them. Joe came back, out of breath. "I don't see any tracks but Bunny's," he

164

reported. "I called, but nobody answered. It's getting too dark to see much."

In spite of the dusk, several of the men set out in the direction from which Bunny had come. Those left at camp could hear their voices calling and see their lanterns swinging through the woods.

"I don't believe Bunny would ever have left Old Andy if he was all right," Uncle Boss said. "The old man must have met with an accident, or . . ."

"There's no use expecting the worst," said Mrs. Kinnery. "Come and get your supper, all of you. Old Andy will probably come marching along before you're through."

But Old Andy did not come. Chief John came over to help with the search, and Jeff and Joe went out with him. They stumbled about the forest until long past their bedtime. When he brought them back they were hoarse from calling, and very sad. The dogs lay down thankfully. They were glad to rest, but they kept their eyes open so that they would not miss anything. The boys felt the same way. "We *can't* go to bed!" they told their mother. "Not until we find Old Andy."

"Oh yes, you can. You have to go to school tomorrow."

"Oh, *no,* Mamma!"

"Oh, yes. The men will start out early in the morning, and they may not get back for several days. The best thing you boys can do is to go to school as usual."

Jeff started to argue. But when he saw his mother turn back to the stove he changed his mind. Here it was past midnight, and she was busy cooking and putting up food for the men to take with them tomorrow. "All right, Mamma," Jeff said.

Joe was wondering how he could slip away and go with the men. He felt that he was too big to have to stay home with the women and children! But when he saw Jeff get back to work on the unpeeled potatoes, while Mrs. Kinnery lifted the heavy water bucket, he took it from her hand.

"Thank you, boys," she smiled.

Jeff and Joe and Maggie went to school next day, but their hearts were not in it. They could not keep their eyes on their books. They kept looking out of the window and thinking about Old Andy, somewhere up on Snow Mountain. A searching party was climbing the mountain now, hoping to find the old prospector. Jeff kept hearing Old Andy's words, "Bunny won't leave me until I'm dead."

During the next few days the logging camp and Chief John's farm were crowded with people who had come to hunt for Old Andy. Foresters, Indians, townspeople came and went at all hours of the day and night. Boss Kinnery and his men came back without finding a clue to Old Andy's whereabouts. Boss left that group at camp to rest, and set out again with another group of lumberjacks to search the other side of the mountain. This time he was gone almost a week.

The townspeople trailed back through the camp and went home. The foresters returned, just as unsuccessful. At last Boss came back, his face sunburned and unshaven. "It's no use," he said. "The old fellow's gone. If he were alive, we would have found him. We've wired his nephew in the East that Old Andy's dead."

Gloom fell on Kinnery Camp. But the work had to go on. The trees had to be felled and the logs had to be floated down to the mill. From dawn to dark the axes rang. Until the timber was sold everyone was on short rations.

17

MR. BEAN

ONE EVENING, just as they were sitting down to supper, a knock was heard at the cookhouse door. Jeff went to open it. A man stood there, dressed in town clothes—a long overcoat with a fur collar, a derby hat, and shiny pointed shoes. "I'd like to speak to Mr. Kinnery," he said.

Boss Kinnery came to the door. "Come in," he invited. "You're just in time for supper."

"Oh, I must not intrude," said the stranger. "I am Andrew Bean. When you notified me of my uncle's death, I came West at once to settle his affairs."

"You're Old Andy's nephew? Glad to meet you, Mr. Bean. I doubt if Old Andy had many affairs to settle, but we'll help you all we can. Come on in, now, and

168

have something to eat."

Mr. Bean took off his coat and hat and gave them to Jeff. He allowed himself to be led to the table. "I wouldn't *think* of imposing on you," he said. "Well, I'll just sit down to be sociable. I really can't eat a thing." He sat down and Joe brought him a well-filled plate. Mr. Bean lifted his fork. "Well, if you *insist—*"

He looked very well fed already, but when he put his knife and fork to work he acted as if he had not eaten for days. Even the lumberjacks, who were hearty eaters themselves, stopped to watch Mr. Bean shovel the food down his throat. Every time a platter was passed or the coffee pot went around, Mr. Bean re-filled his plate or cup. "Well, just a *small* helping," he would say. "If you *insist—*"

When the men left for their bunks and Mrs. Kinnery and the boys sat down for their supper, Mr. Bean continued to eat. "Well, just to be sociable," he said, taking a third helping of pie. His round face shone with pleasure, and his jaws moved steadily. Jeff whispered to Joe, "He's not a bit like Old Andy." Joe whispered back, "Maybe it's because he lives in the East. Maybe he doesn't get cooking like Mamma's very often."

Mrs. Kinnery and the boys cleared the table and set to work on the dishes. Mr. Bean had to stop eating then, since there was nothing left to eat. He pushed his chair back from the table. "Now, shall we talk business, Mr. Kinnery?" he said.

"All right," Uncle Boss agreed, setting himself comfortably. "But I don't know much about Old Andy's business. The only property I ever heard of his owning was the tract of timber across the river that he deeded to me."

Mr. Bean nodded. "That's the very thing I had in mind. That's a valuable piece of property, and as my uncle's heir, I have always expected to inherit it when he died."

Uncle Boss sat up straight. "I am sorry, Mr. Bean, but Old Andy signed the property over to me. You see, I have grubstaked him for twenty years, and he wanted to pay me back."

Mr. Bean's eyebrows went up. The corners of his mouth went down. "Now, really, Mr. Kinnery, do you expect me to believe that? Is anyone going to give away a tract of valuable timber to pay for a few sacks of flour and sides of bacon? The idea is ridiculous!"

Uncle Boss turned red. His hair, already red, stood up on end. "Now look here, Mr. Bean, are you saying that I am not telling the truth? Old Andy *did* give me the timber. His reasons were good enough for him, and they ought to be good enough for you."

"Can you prove it?" Mr. Bean sat smiling his well-fed smile.

170

Boss Kinnery sprang to his feet. "Of course I can prove it. Old Andy wrote out a paper and signed it, right here on this table. I'll show it to you." He stamped off to his room.

They heard him moving in his room, banging drawers and slamming doors. In a moment he bellowed, "Polly!" Mrs. Kinnery hurried to him, wiping her hands on her apron. Again came the sounds of drawers opening and shutting. Mrs. Kinnery came to the door. "Jeff! Joe! Come here a minute."

Jeff and Joe hurried into Uncle Boss's room. Their uncle was standing in the middle of the floor, looking around him wildly. Their mother seemed worried. "Boys," she asked them, "you remember the paper Old Andy signed, giving the timber to Uncle Boss?"

They nodded. "Yes, ma'am."

"Well, Uncle Boss put it in an old wallet that he kept on the closet shelf. Now he can't find the wallet. Do either of you remember seeing it anywhere?"

Jeff and Joe shook their heads. "No, ma'am." They knew how serious this was. If Uncle Boss could not find the paper, he could not prove that he owned the timber, and Mr. Bean would claim that it belonged to him. "We'll help you look for it, Uncle Boss," Jeff said.

Uncle Boss turned on them, sputtering. "You kids keep out of this!" he cried. "How do I know you didn't take the wallet yourselves to make snowshoes for one

of those dratted dogs? I've had nothing but bad luck
since you kids came here. Go away! Get out of my
sight!"

The boys left the room. They heard their mother
say, "Now, Boss," but their uncle exploded, "Don't
you 'Now, Boss' me. Nothing on the place is safe with
those kids around, and you know it."

Jeff and Joe passed through the kitchen, where Mr.
Bean stood warming his hands at the stove with a
satisfied smile. They went to their room and sat on the
edge of their bed, too hurt and angry to say anything.
They heard the search going on for a while; then they
heard Uncle Boss slam out of the house. They heard
Mrs. Kinnery making Mr. Bean comfortable with a cot
by the kitchen stove. The house grew quiet.

172

Finally Joe spoke. "We'll show him! Let's get out of here."

"Mamma will feel bad," said Jeff.

"She feels bad, anyway. Uncle Boss will look out for Mamma. He never gets mad at her, only at us."

"That's so. All right, let's go." Jeff stood up, looking for his jacket.

Joe stopped him. "Wait. We'll have to have to take something to eat."

They selected some things from the storeroom shelves. "We'd better take a water bag—we can fill it up later. And roll up a couple of blankets."

"We'll need matches. And a frying pan."

When their supplies were all piled on the bed, Joe shook his head. "I don't believe we can carry it all."

"I know what!" whispered Jeff. "Let's take Bunny to help us. He doesn't belong to anybody now, so nobody will care."

"That's a good idea. Bring your bundle and we'll go out to the corral and get him."

As quietly as possible they slipped out of the back door. Jasper and Husky followed them. Outside they found Toby crouched at the side of the house, lying in wait for the pack rat. Joe called softly, but he would not budge from his place.

The boys went past the dark bunkhouses, past the blacksmith's shop and around the barn. Bunny came to

173

meet them. Joe put a cord around his neck and led him out. "We'll carry our things until we get away from the camp," he told Jeff. "We can make him a pack later."

"We can't lead him back past the cookhouse," Jeff said. "We'd better go straight through the woods to the river, then circle around behind Chief John's farm."

Joe pulled Bunny forward. "I don't suppose it matters *where* we go," he said gloomily. "Just so we keep out of sight."

They stumbled down the hill to the trail along the creek leading to the river. The walking was easier there. Bunny stepped out briskly, seeming glad to be on his way again. The boys felt very sad, but they, too, were glad to get away from the camp, which Uncle Boss thought was no place for kids. Everything they did seemed to make Uncle Boss mad. Even the things they *didn't* do! The only thing they could do to please him was to get out of his way.

They could hear the river ahead, so they forded the creek and followed the sound of the river in the direction of Snow Mountain. Joe had been thinking as they walked, and presently he said, "If we try to circle behind Chief John's farm, we'll be sure to rouse the dogs. It would be better to keep on along the river. That way we'll be traveling around the foot of the

174

mountain instead of climbing. And we'll keep away from roads and towns."

"All right," Jeff agreed. He was getting tired and sleepy. The dogs were tired, too. They moped at Bunny's heels, hanging their heads. Joe was as tired as any of them, but he kept on and on. After several hours they almost fell into a steep little canyon. The night had grown darker as the hours passed. The chill had got into their bones.

"This is as good a place as any," Joe said. "Nobody will see a fire down in here, if we keep it small. Here, give me the rope. I'll hobble Bunny so he can graze."

They tried to build a fire, but they could not see well enough to find dry wood. "I don't need a fire," Jeff said crossly. "I just want to go to sleep." So, unrolling their blankets, they lay down on the cold earth. The boys lay close together for warmth. Jasper and Husky curled up beside them, and they all fell asleep.

18

ON SNOW MOUNTAIN

WHEN JEFF awoke, the sun was already high in the sky. But it was hidden by thick layers of cloud, so that the morning was as cold and wet and dreary as possible. He sat up and looked around him, trying to remember what had happened.

Joe lay beside him. Bunny was cropping the frosty grass on the bank of the river, foaming over the rocks at the bottom of the narrow canyon. Tall trees grew up the rocky walls, shading the place still further from the light of day. Little streams of melting snow-water tumbled down the cracks in the rocks. The whole canyon was filled with the sound of rushing water. As he looked, Jeff remembered Mr. Bean, the lost deed to Old Andy's timber, and Uncle Boss's unkind words.

176

He remembered that he and Joe were running away.

Joe turned over and opened his eyes. "Let's build a fire and get something to eat," he said.

As they ate, Jeff asked, "Do you think they will hunt for us, Joe?"

"Sure they will. But they'll look for us in town. They'll never guess we went into the woods."

"What will we do when our food runs out?"

"I figure it will last us till we get to the mill. If we stay with the river we ought to reach the mill in a couple of days. Maybe we can get a job there."

The dogs, hearing their voices, came up to say good morning. They had been out hunting, and seemed to have satisfied their hunger. "Well, let's load up Bunny and get going," Joe said.

They caught the burro and tied their blanket-rolls on his back. They unfastened his hobbled legs and made ready to set out. Bunny broke into his funny stiff-legged trot. The boys followed him. They did not notice at first that Bunny was gradually getting farther and farther ahead of them.

Suddenly Jeff asked, "Where's Bunny? He's gone!"

"He must have turned a corner there beyond the rocks," Joe said. "Hey, Bunny! Whoa, there; whoa!"

When they rounded the corner themselves, they looked down the river, expecting to see Bunny there. But he wasn't. Looking all around, they caught sight

177

of the burro climbing like a mountain goat up a ravine that led back into the mountains. "Hey, Bunny!" they called. "Come back here this minute!" Hey!"

But Bunny just trotted on faster up the mountain.

"We can't let him go!" Joe cried. "He's got everything we own on his back. Come on! We ought to be able to catch him."

They scrambled up the ravine after Bunny, calling out to him as they went. The dogs, excited by the chase, began to bark. Old Jasper raised his deep voice.

"They'll hear us all over the Reservation," Joe said. They slowed down to a walk and stopped calling out. The dogs fell back, and Bunny, looking over his shoulder, saw that he was no longer being pursued. He

stopped on a steep slope and nibbled at a patch of moss.

"He's waiting for us. If we're real quiet we can get close to him," said Jeff.

Sure enough, Bunny waited until they almost caught up. But just as they reached out for him he leaped upward and went on climbing.

Joe lost his temper. He picked up a rock and threw it at the burro. Of course, this only caused Bunny to climb the faster. The boys stood, catching their breath. "We never should have let him loose," Joe admitted.

"But Andy never led him. He said Bunny could find a trail better than he could. He said Bunny *never* ran away."

"Well, he's gone now. If we follow him we'll have to do a lot of climbing. But if we go on without him, we won't have anything to camp with. Even the matches are tied up in my blanket-roll."

Jeff complained, "And I'm getting hungry already. Let's follow him, Joe! He'll get tired pretty soon and let us catch him."

Joe looked doubtfully up the mountain. "Once we lose sight of the river it will be easy to get lost."

"It doesn't matter where we go, anyway. And we can always find the river again if we want to by going downhill."

"Well, all right."

They followed Bunny for hours. He seemed almost to be playing a game with them. Whenever they grew tired and were ready to give up, Bunny would stop and wait for them, grazing peacefully. As they came closer, he would twitch one ear forward and one ear back. Sometimes he would turn his head and gaze at them and nod in a friendly way. The boys would think, "Now, we've got him!" Then, with a swish of his tail, Bunny would bounce off again just like the animal he was named for.

Jeff and Joe paid little attention to where they were

180

going. After the rough climb up the ravine, they found themselves in a forest of pine, under which thickets of vine maple made it difficult to keep Bunny in view. Several times they lost him altogether, but the dogs usually found him for them. Once, however, they were led off by the dogs, only to discover that they were following a deer instead of a donkey. Retracing their steps as best they could, they came upon Bunny again, enjoying a meal of dry fern.

The higher they went, the colder grew the air, but exercise kept them from feeling the chill. Up the slopes, over the ridges, up ravines and around shoulders of rock they went. They could not see ahead any distance because of the trees. There was no sun to tell time by. But at last they realized that it was growing dark. The day was drawing to a close, and Jeff and Joe were lost somewhere high on Snow Mountain.

Neither of them spoke for a long time. They were tired and hungry, and ashamed of themselves for getting into such a fix. But they couldn't go on walking all night. Joe broke the silence. "It looks like we're getting to the top of a ridge. When we come to a clear space, we might as well stop for the night."

They trudged on until they topped the ridge. Surprisingly, the big trees ended at the top, and they could look out over a tremendous expanse of country. Straight ahead of them rose the main peak of Snow

181

Mountain, white as a ghost above the timberline. Between them and the peak lay miles of rough hills and valleys, forests, creeks, and canyons. They could not see any of the places they knew. Kinnery Camp, the Agency, Battle Ridge, the farm, and the river had all disappeared. They seemed to have wandered into a different world.

A cold wind off the snow fields brought their attention back to the problem of making camp for the night. Just over the ridge, right at their feet, lay a tiny mountain meadow like a shallow bowl. A windbreak of young fir trees offered some shelter on the side toward the mountain. Not far below them they could hear running water.

"This would be a good camping place," Joe said, "if only we had our packs!"

"Look!" pointed Jeff.

There was Bunny at the edge of the meadow. In the dusk they had not noticed him at first, for his gray hide blended into the background of dark firs. "You go around on the other side," Joe whispered. "I'll come at him from this side. We've *got* to catch him this time!"

Jeff crept through the little fir trees, trying to move as silently as the Indians he had read about. He did manage to be very quiet, for Bunny's ear did not even twitch as Jeff peeped out at him between the branches.

183

Jeff waited until he saw Joe walking slowly across the meadow. He moved one foot forward, then waited to see if Bunny were looking. Then he moved another step. Foot by foot he came almost within arm's reach of the burro without frightening him.

"Now!" cried Joe. Jeff pounced out of the thicket and fell upon Bunny's neck. At the same time Joe grabbed Bunny. They both clung to the beast, hugging him as if they never intended to let him go.

"I can't believe it," Jeff sighed. "We've got him! We've got him! Let me at that bacon and beans!"

Joe pulled Bunny's long whiskery ears. "We're going to tie you up before we do anything else," he told him.

Bunny was hobbled that night, and in addition was fastened to a stake by a length of rope. As for the boys, they ate a hearty supper, warmed themselves by a fire, and fell thankfully asleep with Jasper and Husky beside them.

19

THE RESCUE

IT WAS SO COLD that night that Jeff and Joe had
to take turns getting up to keep the fire burning. The
wind off of Snow Mountain grew steadily more bitter.
By morning it was carrying gusts of fine snowflakes.

The boys ate a good breakfast in spite of their discomfort, for they knew that they must eat to keep going. But their supply of food was getting low.

While they ate they considered what they should do.
It was plain enough that they must get back to civiliza-
tion as soon as they could. But where should they go?
They did not know where they were. They could still
see the peak of Snow Mountain, but they were not at
all sure which side of it they were on. To make matters
worse, the gusts of snow were coming closer together.

At first they had thought that the wind was just blowing loose snow from the mountain. Now it began to look as if it was new snow, the beginning of a storm.

"Well, which way shall we go?" They looked out over the wide landscape, searching for something to set their direction by. The wind made them blink their eyes, and curtains of flying snow blotted out more and more of the view as they watched.

Bunny tugged at his rope, pointing his ears forward and prancing as if he were eager to set out again. "Oh, no, you don't!" Joe told him. "No more of your follow-the-leader games. We'll all stick together from now on."

"Look there!" cried Jeff suddenly.

"Where?"

"Over there—just below the timberline on the peak."

"I don't see anything. What is it?"

Jeff sighed. "I don't either, now. I guess it wasn't anything. I thought I saw some smoke."

Joe looked where he pointed. "I see it. But it's just the snow blowing around. No, wait. It's blue. I believe it *is* smoke, Jeff!"

They strained their eyes, gazing at the faraway forest-covered slope of the mountain. For a moment the wind shifted, giving a clear view of a tiny column of blue smoke rising above the trees. The column broke into puffs. Puff! puff! puff! Then the view was wiped out by

186

a flurry of stinging snow. The boys were jubilant.

"It *is* smoke! What's more, it's a smoke signal. Somebody's over there."

The dogs and Bunny seemed to feel their excitement. The whole party started out at full speed; Jasper barking, Husky frisking, Bunny snorting, and the boys marching along full of hope. They could not keep up such a pace long, for there was a great deal of space to be covered. Soon they had to settle down to a steady walk.

Although the snow flurries continued all day, the threatened storm held off. As Jeff and Joe plodded doggedly uphill and down, fording streams and skirting canyons, wandering through dense forests, they were able from time to time to check their directions from some high point of view. Gradually they drew nearer to the snow-clad peak, and could see trees and rocks in the neighborhood of the smoke. For the smoke still rose. Sometimes it was just a feeble thread, snatched away by the wind, but always it came back. Several times the boys saw the signal repeated, Puff! puff! puff!

It gave them hope. Without it, Jeff thought, he would not have been able to keep moving. He had never been so tired in his life. Nor so cold. Nor so homesick. "I wouldn't even mind peeling potatoes!" he muttered. He did not know he had spoken out loud,

188

but Joe heard him, in spite of his own discomfort.

"I wouldn't either," Joe admitted. He had been thinking of Kinnery Camp, too. He would have given anything to see the people there again, even Maggie. He looked at Jeff and saw how tired he was. "Look, why don't you ride Bunny for awhile?"

"I will if you'll take turns with me," Jeff said. Had he and Joe ever quarreled about who would ride Schoolboy? It didn't seem possible. If they ever got home safely, Jeff promised himself, he would *never* quarrel with Joe again.

They were too tired to wonder what they would find when they reached the smoke. They just stumbled on. They took turns riding and leading Bunny. Bunny never seemed to get tired. He stepped along briskly, choosing his footholds carefully. When the boys stopped to rest or eat he would not graze, but tugged at his rope and pointed his ears up the mountain.

Late in the afternoon they were climbing the slopes of the peak itself. They were among the big trees again, and had no chance to see where they were going. All they knew was that they were going up. Suddenly Joe realized that Bunny, instead of being led, was leading *him*. Tired as he was, he did not try to hold the animal back. He hung on to the rope and followed as best he could. The dogs lagged at his heels, stopping often to lick their sore paws. Jeff was half-asleep between the

189

blanket-rolls on Bunny's back, not knowing where he was.

He was waked with a shock by a loud noise. His comfortable seat was shaking so that he almost fell off of Bunny's back. Bunny was braying, "Hee-haw! Hee-haw!"

Joe and the dogs came up and they all paused to look at the scene before them. Almost at their feet the ground fell away. A long, narrow lake lay below, its glassy waters reflecting the trees and the snowy peak beyond. Looking straight down into the clear water from the overhanging rock on which they stood, the boys saw the gaunt, bare branches of dead trees reaching up toward them.

"Lost Valley Lake!" Jeff exclaimed. He was standing on the very spot Chief John had told him about. He was seeing what the ancient chief's son had seen so long ago.

Joe did know what Jeff meant, and for the moment he did not care. His attention was caught by a small log cabin half-hidden by trees. It seemed to be built against the rocky wall of the mountain itself. A column of blue smoke rose from its chimney.

Jeff looked where Joe pointed. Both boys drew a deep breath. The smell of burning juniper spiced the air. "Hee-haw! Hee-haw!" Bunny made the echoes ring. Catching Joe off guard, the burro pulled the rope

from his grasp and made full speed toward the cabin. Jeff, unseated, tumbled to the ground with a thump.

He picked himself up and ran with Joe and the dogs after Bunny. Bunny pushed at the door of the cabin with his nose. It swung open and the boys looked in.

It was dark inside, but a fire burning in a stone fireplace gave a flickering light. By its ruddy glow they could see a man lying in a bunk built on the wall. Only his head stuck out from the heap of bedclothes. They made out his white hair, white whiskers, and bright blue eyes. It was Old Andy.

He smiled at them feebly. "Come in, come in!" he said. His voice was very weak.

"Andy! What's the matter, Andy? Are you sick? Are you hurt?" Jeff and Joe went to the bunk. The old man got his hand out from under the covers and patted their shoulders as they bent over him.

"I got under a falling rock at the wrong time. Crushed my foot. Silly thing for an old crag rat like me to do. Where did you boys come from? When Bunny didn't come back I figured folks had given me up for dead."

Jeff told him, "That's just what happened, Andy. Uncle Boss and everybody hunted for you for days and days. They finally did give up."

"Then how did you boys get here?"

"Bunny brought us."

"But why—"

Joe interrupted. He had been looking around the cabin. The food supplies looked plentiful, but there were few signs of cooking and eating. "You haven't been able to feed yourself, have you, Andy?" he asked.

"I did all right at first. But then the fever came. And I saved all my strength to keep the fire going, in case someone might see the smoke."

"You've got to have something to eat," Joe said. "Come on, Jeff, let's get busy."

They built up the fire and prepared a bountiful meal. After their cold nights on the wild, wet mountain, they were happy to be in a warm cabin, with a roaring fire and a table loaded with hot food. Before they ate, however, they saw to it that Bunny was safely housed in his lean-to shed at the side of the cabin. The snow was falling in earnest now, driving out of the night as if it meant to smother their lantern. Dashing back into the cabin, they found Old Andy struggling to get out of bed. His injured foot was an ugly thing, swollen and red.

"None of that, now!" cried Joe. He pushed him back into the bunk, propped him up, and began to feed him. They could almost see the strength coming back into him with the food.

The dogs lay on the hearth, full of food and contentment. When Old Andy was fed, Jeff and Joe sat down to the table. All the time they had been lost they had not told each other how scared they were. But now that it was over, they looked at each other and grinned.

"I'll never forget how you boys rescued me!" Old Andy murmured.

The boys grinned more widely. "And *we'll* never forget how you rescued *us!*" Jeff said.

20

THE RETURN

OLD ANDY was propped up in his bunk wide awake when the boys woke up next morning. They all ate an enormous breakfast, and then Old Andy said, "I been thinking during the night while my foot was hurting bad. I've got to get to a doctor before it's too late. Now, there's no use sending you boys to bring the doctor here. You might get lost, and anyway, it would take twice as long that way. The only thing to do is for me to go to the doctor."

Jeff said, "There's an awful lot of snow." He had been out to the woodpile, and had gone in over his knees.

"It's pretty cold, too," said Joe. "Do you think you could make it, even riding on Bunny?"

195

"I can try," Old Andy said. "There isn't near as much snow farther down the mountain, and Bunny knows every step of the way. Even if I go off my head with fever, Bunny will lead us in. You fellows will have to help me on and off the burro, and maybe even hold me on, if I get bad."

Joe shook his head. "I don't know, Andy. I don't know if you can make it."

"You just get me wrapped up good and warm," ordered Old Andy. "I'll show you if I can make it!"

They followed his directions, and brought him all his warmest clothes. They finished by cutting up some blankets and tying them around his legs and feet. He looked so funny they couldn't help laughing.

"You look almost as fat as your nephew, Mr. Bean!" Jeff laughed.

"What do *you* know about Andrew Bean?" Old Andy asked, surprised. "He lives in the East."

"But he's at the camp right now, Andy. He came to take your timber away from Uncle Boss."

"He came to *what?*" Old Andy's white whiskers stood out like porcupine quills.

"He came to take the timber because you were dead, and he said he was your heir, and everything you had belonged to him." Jeff went on to tell about the loss of the paper which proved that the timber belonged to Uncle Boss, and how their uncle had accused them of taking the wallet and losing it.

"That's why we ran away," Joe explained. "Uncle Boss never did want us at Kinnery Camp, anyway. He said he never wanted to see us again."

Old Andy actually started hopping to the door on his one good foot. "Come on! What are we waiting for?" he cried. "When I get to camp, it won't matter about the paper. I'll show Andrew Bean whether I'm dead or not! Dead or alive, he shan't have that timber."

The journey down the mountain was every bit as bad as they had feared. In spite of all his wrappings, Old Andy was soon shaking from the cold. The snow was so deep that Jeff and Joe and Bunny had all they could do to plow through it. When they stopped to rest

197

they all got so cold that they had to move on at once.

There were some things, though, to be thankful for. At least they were not lost, this time. Although Jeff and Joe did not know the way, Old Andy and Bunny did. They were able to take a much shorter route than the one the boys had come up by. Then, too, the snow did get less deep the further down they went. By the time they stopped for lunch they could look back and see the peak of Snow Mountain already far behind them. Old Andy said that if they kept on going they might get to Kinnery Camp that night.

So they kept on going. They went on and on and on. Late in the day poor Old Andy began to wander in his mind. The boys walked on either side of him, ready to prop him up if he fell. But he stayed on Bunny's back, his long legs dangling. He talked to himself, and sometimes he sang. As the darkness fell, it was enough to scare anybody to death.

Darkness came slowly, because they were still high above the sunset, and had the advantage of the very last light of the sun, although it was hidden behind the clouds. But when night did come, it was the thickest, blackest, most frightening night Jeff had ever known. He could not see anything beyond the small circle of lantern light. There was Bunny with his head down, not even looking where he was going, and stumbling every third step. What if he lost the way, after all? And

198

there was Old Andy, swaying back and forth, muttering to himself like a crazy man. Even the dogs looked
scared, their tails drooping. Jeff wondered if Joe was
as frightened as he was.

Joe was. It was all he could do to keep from running.
He wanted to get down the mountain quick—to get

somewhere where it was warm and light. But he kept on plodding beside Bunny, holding out the lantern that did no good at all. Everything depended on Bunny now. If he lost his way, they would be wandering around in the darkness all night.

After a long time they realized that they were out on the open hillside. They could see some lights quite near below them, and farther away another cluster of lights. Still others, faint but twinkling, showed here and there in the valley. Dogs began to bark. Jasper and Husky answered them.

"I know where we are!" said Jeff suddenly. It had been so long since he had spoken that his own voice sounded strange to him. "We're just above Chief John's farm. There's Kinnery Camp over there!"

Bunny lifted his head and pricked up his ears. Perhaps he smelled the hay in Chief John's barn. At any rate he started to trot. Old Andy slipped sideways and almost fell. It took both the boys to hold him on.

Chief John's voice came out of the night, "Hey, up there! Who is it?"

Jeff and Joe cried out together. Neither of them could manage much more than a squeak. "It's us, Chief John! We've got Old Andy!"

Chief John came charging up the hill. With him were Ole and Fred. At their heels tagged Maggie. The boys tried to say hello to everybody at once. Everyone tried to talk at once, while Old Andy went on babbling to himself. Chief John said, "Run back and ring the bell, Maggie. The folks at the camp are waiting for news."

As they went down the hill Chief John told Jeff and Joe that they had been searching for them ever since they went away. He and Ole and Fred had just come in to eat and change clothes. Uncle Boss and another group were still out, and Mrs. Kinnery was at the camp frantic with worry.

The farmhouse bell was answered at once by the triangle at the camp cookhouse. That was the signal that had been agreed upon in case the boys were found.

Before they knew it Jeff and Joe were back at Kinnery Camp, stumbling up the cookhouse steps into their mother's arms. In no time at all Old Andy was tucked into the cot by the stove, with hot-water bottles all around him and blankets up to his chin. Chief John's son was already off on Home Run to fetch the doctor.

The first thing Jeff noticed when his mother stopped hugging him for a moment was Mr. Bean standing by the cot staring at Old Andy. His mouth was open like a gasping fish.

Toby dashed in, barked and danced around the boys, and dashed out again. He was still guarding the pack-rat hole under the house. Jasper and Husky

201

curled up behind the stove as if they had never been away.

Every so often someone would beat the triangle to call in Uncle Boss and his searching party, and at last they came in, red-eyed and tired. Then it was their turn to stare at Old Andy. The doctor came and dressed the old prospector's foot, and when he said he thought it was going to be all right, the lumberjacks staggered off to their bunks to catch up on their sleep.

"We've all had precious little sleep while you boys were gone!" Boss Kinnery spoke to Jeff and Joe for the first time.

"Now we're in for it," Jeff thought. Joe's lower lip thrust forward, and Mrs. Kinnery's chin went up.

A weak voice spoke from the cot. "Funny how a couple of kids could find me when the grown men had to give up," said Old Andy.

Boss Kinnery nodded. "I've been wondering how they did it," he admitted. "I know what that country is like. I thought we had searched every inch of it, but *we* couldn't find you."

Jeff and Joe looked at each other. What had come over Uncle Boss? But his next words sounded more like himself. He turned to them. "But you should have told us before you struck out like that. We've been scouring the country for you, and your mother has worried herself sick."

202

Again Old Andy spoke for the boys. "They were in a hurry to get your timber back for you."

Uncle Boss turned a fiery red. Not with anger, this time. "I'm sorry I said that about your taking the paper, boys!" he muttered. "I was just out of my head with disappointment."

"That's all right, Uncle Boss," Jeff said. He hated to see anybody uncomfortable. He could tell that Uncle Boss really *was* sorry.

Mrs. Kinnery nudged Joe. He muttered, "Sure."

Uncle Boss went on. "You see, I was counting on that timber. Without it I was just a dead-broke lumberjack. With it I'm the Bull-of-the-Woods! I had some—some special plans, too."

Jeff pricked up his ears. "What plans, Uncle Boss?"

Boss looked at Mrs. Kinnery. She said, "No more questions tonight. Bedtime!"

She didn't need to say it twice. Bed never looked so good to Jeff and Joe.

21

A GOOD PLACE FOR KIDS

NEXT DAY Mr. Bean was gone. Jeff and Joe never knew when he left or where he went, but he was never seen at Kinnery Camp again.

No mention was made of school. Instead, Uncle Boss said, after a late breakfast, "How would you boys like to go into town with your mother and me?"

Uncle Boss was dressed in his very best town clothes. His hair was plastered down and his ears were rosy with scrubbing.

"Aren't you going to work today, Uncle Boss?"

"The men can work without me today," Boss said. "They can even do without me tomorrow. But before we go, I have to ask you fellows a question."

Jeff and Joe looked at him, wondering what was going to come next. He had been so different since they had come back that they hardly knew what to expect.

"You've been at Kinnery Camp almost a year now," Uncle Boss went on. "How do you like it?"

"We like it fine!" Jeff said. Joe nodded. His uncle seemed to be having a hard time saying what he wanted to, and Joe wasn't going to help him.

"Do you like it well enough to stay for good?"

"But you said it was no place for kids!" Jeff reminded him.

Uncle Boss turned red again. "Well, I've changed my mind." He turned still redder. He looked at Mrs. Kinnery, but she was no help. She was blushing too. "Look here," Boss Kinnery blurted out, "if I married your mother, you'd belong to me as much as you do her. I'd *have* to put up with *you* then, and *you'd* have to put up with *me*. Do you think you could?"

Jeff and Joe were surprised at the idea. After a moment's thought, Jeff found that it really seemed very natural. Their mother was watching them anxiously. Jeff smiled, and she smiled back. She looked very young and happy. Jeff said, "Sure we could, Uncle Boss!"

Joe wouldn't look at his mother or Uncle Boss. He didn't know what to say. He really didn't want his mother to marry anybody. Still, he *did* like Kinnery

Camp, and after being lost on Snow Mountain, he wasn't nearly as mad at Uncle Boss as he had been. Mrs. Kinnery asked softly, "How about it, Joe?"

Joe gulped. "I guess it would be all right."

"Hooray!" Old Andy crowed from his cot. His voice was stronger this morning, and his blue eyes twinkled. "Now, for goodness sake, go on to town and get it over with!"

Jeff and Joe had never been to a wedding before. They enjoyed the trip to town, especially staying overnight at a hotel. They did not see why people should make such a fuss over standing up before a preacher and having words said over them. But Uncle Boss and their mother seemed excited and happy about it, and since Uncle Boss had changed his mind about kids, Jeff and Joe were happy too.

On the way back to Kinnery Camp, they stopped at the mill. The river was choked with logs. There were

so many of them and they came down so fast that the river-pigs had all they could do to keep them from jamming the millpond. "Those are our own logs!" Uncle Boss said. "We don't owe a cent on 'em. Don't they look good?"

Mrs. Kinnery and the boys agreed that they did. They would have liked to watch them churning downstream forever, but it was getting late. Regretfully, Mrs. Kinnery said, "We'd better start back to camp, Boss, if we're going to get any supper."

Although she was smiling, the boys knew that she was thinking about that supper she had to cook for thirty men. They themselves were reminded of all the potatoes that would be waiting for them to peel. They almost wished that the team would not go so fast. But of course the team went faster the nearer they came to camp, for they knew they were nearing their barn and their feed. *They* didn't have to think about dishes to wash and potatoes to peel.

The Kinnery family walked back from the barn to the cookhouse. They were all glad to be home. They drew in deep breaths of pine and pine smoke. Jasper and Husky ran circles around them, making them welcome. Toby was still crouched at the side of the house. His eyes rolled toward them and his short tail twitched, but he did not leave his post.

Suddenly Mrs. Kinnery stopped and sniffed. "Some-

body's cooking!" she exclaimed. "Old Andy's not well enough for that. Who can it be?"

As if in answer, a little yellow man came out on the steps. He was smiling all over his round face, making his snapping black eyes almost disappear. He wore a long apron, and held up a big spoon in one hand. "How do! How do!" he chuckled.

"Howdy do," Mrs. Kinnery replied, puzzled.

Boss boomed out, "Polly, this is Wong Lee, our new cook."

Mrs. Kinnery could only stare at him, speechless. The boys jumped up and down with excitement. "Oh, Mamma! You won't have to cook any more! You won't have to work so hard. Oh, Uncle Boss!"

"What are we waiting for?" asked Uncle Boss. He pushed them inside. "Let's see what Lee has fixed for supper."

Just inside the door the boys stopped short. It was their turn to stare, speechless. There sat Old Andy in the rocking chair by the stove, rocking away while he peeled potatoes. He had pans of neatly peeled potatoes all around him.

"Meet the new Bull Cook," Uncle Boss said. "Andy has decided to stay with us and help with the chores from now on, instead of chipping off pieces of Snow Mountain."

Andy grinned, his whiskers curling up on each side of his mouth. "Of course, I'll have to have some help until my foot gets well," he said to the boys. Jeff ran to him and hugged both him and the potatoes. Joe was too big for such behavior, but he spoke up along with Jeff, promising to help him all he wanted.

"We'll do our share, won't we, boys?" Mrs. Kinnery joined in. "Just imagine sitting down to a meal that somebody else has cooked!"

"And no dishes to wash afterward!" cried Joe.

Uncle Boss beamed. Lee bobbed his head up and

down and chuckled. Old Andy rocked back and forth like a steam engine.

"Let's not imagine it—let's do it!" Uncle Boss said.

"Run and wash your hands, boys." Mrs. Kinnery wouldn't forget to tell them that, no matter what happened.

The supper table was heaped with good things. There were baked potatoes and fried potatoes. There was fried chicken and fried ham and big puffy biscuits and pickles and cake and cookies and canned corn and tomatoes and peaches and apple pie. The men crowded into the room. They each had a word and a joke for the newlyweds, but their eyes were fixed on all the good things to eat.

They all sat down at the table. Uncle Boss was at the head, with Jeff on one side of him and Joe on the other. They could look down the long table to Mrs. Kinnery at the other end. She looked back at them and smiled over all the fine food that she had not cooked. Lee smiled at everyone. The only time he frowned was when somebody's plate was empty. He wouldn't let a plate stay empty even for a minute.

Just as supper was nearly over—because everyone had eaten all he possibly could—a dreadful commotion broke out under the house. "That's Toby!" cried Joe. "He must have finally got that pack rat he's been waiting for."

"Well, thank goodness. I won't have to hear him gnawing under my room any more," said Uncle Boss. "Go let Toby in and feed him. He hasn't eaten anything for days."

Joe went to the door and opened it. Toby burst into the room and went prancing across the floor toward

Uncle Boss. He was carrying something in his mouth, and wagging his stump of a tail as fast as it would go.

"What's that he has in his mouth, Boss?" Mrs. Kinnery asked. "Don't you dare let him bring that pack rat in here. I don't care how proud of it he is."

Toby rolled his eyes at her reproachfully.

"It's not the rat." Uncle Boss took the object from Toby's mouth and turned it over and over. "It's that wallet I lost, with Andy's paper in it."

"Well, I declare! So it was the pack rat that carried it away! We should have thought of that."

Uncle Boss looked at the boys. "*I* should have thought of it, before I said what I did."

Jeff and Joe hung on to either side of his chair, looking at the wallet. It was gnawed a little on the corners, but the paper inside was not spoiled.

"If only he had brought it in a little sooner!" sighed Mrs. Kinnery.

"Oh, but I'm glad he didn't!" cried Jeff. "If he had, Joe and I wouldn't have run away, and we wouldn't have found Andy—and Uncle Boss wouldn't have changed his mind about kids."

"Then I'm glad, too," said Mrs. Kinnery.

"Me too!" said Joe.

"Well, I'm gladdest of all," said Boss Kinnery.

"How about me?" demanded Old Andy.

The door opened and in marched Mac playing his pipes. Ole and Fred and Chub and Little Shorty and Big Shorty marched behind him, breaking into a jig now and then. Bunny, in the corral, brayed so loud that he almost drowned out the music. Jasper and Husky began to howl, and Toby barked. Just when one would think there couldn't be any more noise, a new sound joined in. Lee brought out an outlandish-looking flute. He sat on the edge of the woodbox and blew on it, producing the most earsplitting sounds.

Mrs. Kinnery threw up her hands. She had laughed until she was out of breath. "What a place! What a place!" she gasped.

"It's a good place!" Jeff cried. "Isn't it, Joe?"

"Sure it is."

"It *is* a good place," Uncle Boss agreed, looking all around. "It's a *good* place for kids."